Suspense

STA   Stashower, Daniel o.

The adventure of the
ectoplasmic man

THE ADVENTURE OF THE ECTOPLASMIC MAN

THE
ADVENTURE
OF THE
ECTOPLASMIC
MAN

DANIEL STASHOWER

WILLIAM MORROW AND COMPANY, INC.

New York

Grateful acknowledgment is made to Dame Jean Conan Doyle for
permission to use characters created by Sir Arthur Conan Doyle.

Library of Congress Cataloging in Publication Data

Stashower, Daniel.
The adventure of the ectoplasmic man.

1. Houdini, Harry, 1874–1926—Fiction. I. Title.
PS3569.T33635A68   1985   813′.54   84-20552
ISBN-0-688-04189-2

Printed in the United States of America

First Edition

1 2 3 4 5 6 7 8 9 10

BOOK DESIGN BY ELLEN LO GIUDICE

*For David
and
Sally*

ACKNOWLEDGMENTS

The author wishes to thank the following people for their invaluable help and guidance: Evan and Anne Thomas, Doug Stumpf, Peter Shepherd, Frank MacShane and the Tuesday Club, Stephen Koch, Joseph Epstein, Jon Appleton, Lillian Zevin, Nicholas Meyer, The Book Ranger, Richard Ruhlman, Marta Panajoth, Sara Stashower, Rachel Weintraub, Fred and Hildegarde, Emily, The John Beach family and especially its Manhattan satellite, Chip Tucker, Harold the green pig, Jack Berman, and Miss Ellen O'Neill Beach.

ACKNOWLEDGMENTS

CONTENTS

EDITOR'S FOREWORD

I was not the one who discovered the note from John H. Watson to Bess Houdini, but I was the first to recognize that John H. Watson was not the John Watson from Nebraska, who juggled meat hooks, but the famous *Dr.* John H. Watson, biographer and companion of Sherlock Holmes.

It happened shortly after the death of Al Grasso, when we members of the New York City Society of American Magicians began sorting through the accumulated clutter in his shop, The Grasso-Hornmann Magic Company. Grasso's was, and is, New York's most peculiar landmark. It is the oldest magic store in America, and the spiritual birthplace of many of our greatest magicians. In almost any other magic store in the country you'll find the magic enclosed in glass cases. Not so at Grasso's. At Grasso's you dive into the tricks as you would a pile of leaves. It's not so much a store as a museum, a dim warehouse on the second floor of an old office building, where printed silks and tasseled wands and huge metal hoops are all jumbled together and randomly stuffed into boxes and onto shelves. The place is full of magic books and pamphlets, some of them very rare, none of them in any kind of order. In one corner is a scarred leather-top desk where Al Grasso kept his records, such as they were, and hanging above it there are more than one hundred sepia photographs of the great vaudeville magicians. And when the sun is shining in through the back window, you can catch a glimpse of some huge stage illusion among the stacks of packing crates—the corner of The Mummy's Asrah, or the golden tail of The Chinese Dragon —relics of the great full-evening magic shows of the 1920s and '30s.

It's a wonder that anybody ever found anything of use in all that dust and clutter, but every year thousands of magicians would come—beginners and professionals—and each of them would uncover the one book, trick, or memento which he had always wanted and had never been able to find.

Straightening the place out, then, even with the best of intentions. was a sad, almost blasphemous task. We took our slow and deferential time about it, allowing the older members time to pause over each piece of memorabilia and tell stories of the old days. Working in this fashion, we did not begin excavating Al Grasso's desk until the third afternoon, and in the process uncovered a brittle, coffee-stained manila envelope marked "Return to Bess Houdini."

It was like hearing sleigh bells on Christmas Eve. We all knew that Al Grasso had been a close friend of Mrs. Houdini. We also knew that sometime during the First World War Grasso's, then called Martinka's, had been owned by Harry Houdini. But most of us regarded Houdini as something of a mythical figure, and it just didn't seem possible that we could be holding an envelope, an envelope with coffee stains on it, meant to be given to his wife. Maybe it was something that had belonged to Houdini, we thought. Maybe it was the plans to an escape. The whole group of us, about seven that afternoon, stared at the envelope for about five minutes before someone finally dumped the contents out onto the newly cleared desktop.

The first item we examined did a lot to dispel our reverence. It was a photograph of Houdini and a friend, in which the great magician, unaware he was being photographed full length, was standing on his toes to appear taller than the other man. The Great Houdini was embarrassed about his height!

There were more pictures in the envelope, mostly of Houdini and other, shorter magicians. And there were letters to and from Houdini concerning the sale of Martinka's. And finally, there was a small piece of yellowed notepaper which had fallen to the floor and went unnoticed until Matt the Mindreader picked it up, read it, said, "Huh! The meat hook man!" and passed it to me. The note read:

12 December 1927
Dear Mrs. Houdini,

Again let me extend my warmest sympathies for the loss of your husband. I know what it is to lose a cherished spouse, and can well appreciate that the long months since his passing have done little to ease your grief. Under separate cover I am sending my chronicle of the adventure we shared in London, some twenty years ago now. Though I have no intention at present of making the facts public, I flatter myself that the account of your husband's remarkable exploits may bring some pleasure to you in these unhappy times. I remain,

Your Humble Servant,
John H. Watson

For the second time that day I felt the thrill of discovering a tangible link to one of my idols, and even more astonishingly, evidence that Sherlock Holmes and Harry Houdini had actually met! No sooner had I considered this possibility than an even more incredible one occurred to me: Perhaps somewhere in the store lay an unpublished Watson manuscript!

As I recall it, I explained this possibility to my friends in my usual measured, sonorous tones. They insist I shouted like a madman. Either way, we began a frantic, reckless search for the manuscript in the darkest recesses of Grasso's. All the while I tried not to think of how slim the chances of finding it were. Even if Watson's manuscript had arrived at Martinka's, it would almost surely have been forwarded, discarded, or lost forever in the jumble that became Grasso's. But at that moment we were all too caught up in the search to worry about any of that. We must have looked like the Keystone Kops, diving into stacks of papers, dumping out cartons of documents, and rifling through the files; not missing a trick, as it were. Manuscripts were uncovered and hastily scanned, only to be revealed as treatises on dove vanishing or coin manipulation. Then, miraculously, after only twenty minutes or so, we found Dr. Watson's manuscript. It had been serving as a shim under the unsteady leg of a goldfish vanish table. Ignominious as this may seem, it probably saved the manuscript from being thrown out.

The bundle was in fairly good condition, apart from the sinkhole where the table leg had rested. The first few pages were on the point of crumbling and the last few were stained with oil or grease, but all of it was legible. I know this because I immediately sat down and read straight through while my friends tried to repair the damage done by our search. If possible, Grasso's was now even more disordered than when we began cleaning it three days before, and we then abandoned all hope of restoring it to order; but I had an original, unpublished Sherlock Holmes story.

That's where my troubles really began. If discovering a Watson manuscript seemed unlikely, convincing the world of the discovery bordered on the impossible. I faced an army of disbelievers. To begin with, the skeptics said, the writing was not Watson's; but surely he would not, at the age of seventy-five, have made his own longhand copies.

Then there were those who doubted that he would have gone to the trouble of writing the story merely to cheer up Mrs. Houdini. I can only answer that that is exactly the sort of man he was. Furthermore, in 1927 Watson had no real need of money and would have been able to pursue whatever writing appealed to him.

Though this case is unique among Holmes adventures, it was not the first time that Watson kept a completed story under wraps for reasons of discretion. His chief concern would have been to avoid embarrassing the august person involved in the episode. Whatever his reasons, Watson succumbed to viral pneumonia within two years of his note to Mrs. Houdini. Surely Holmes took no interest in the project, so any hope of the story coming to light died with Watson.

No sooner were these objections answered than new ones were raised. Some people even went so far as to accuse me of having written the story myself, despite my assurances that I am an untalented boor. Then there was that contemptible faction that insists that Sherlock Holmes existed only in the mind of Sir Arthur Conan Doyle. They are a spurious lot, surely, but they comprise a large faction in the publishing industry and therefore could not be ignored. Finally, after many months of effort, I was able to convince William Morrow and Company, a sympathetic publishing house, that, however dubious the origin of the manuscript might be, it was still a damn good story. I leave it to the reader to make the final judgment. I myself have no doubts, and I assure the reader that the most fantastic assertions and events herein are the most easily verified. The episode related by Bess Houdini in Chapter Three is retold by Milbourne Christopher in his biography, *Houdini: The Untold Story*. The escape introduced by Houdini in the Epilogue became a standard feature in his stage show; and he recreated the amazing stunt described in the nineteenth chapter in the movie *The Grim Game*.

I have made a few awkward but, I hope, illuminating footnotes in those places where Watson's notorious murkiness asserts itself, but otherwise I will intrude no further on the reader's patience. Watson is in good form as always, a friend to the reader and the one fixed point in a changing age. . . .

Daniel Stashower
New York City
February 12, 1985

AUTHOR'S FOREWORD

In all my years with Sherlock Holmes I encountered only a handful of men whose wilfulness and ingenuity rivalled that of Holmes himself. One such man was William Gladstone, the late prime minister. Another was a gentleman in Cornwall who fashioned small weapons from dried fruit. But by far the most extraordinary of these was Harry Houdini, the renowned magician and escape artist.

Sherlock Holmes and Harry Houdini met in April of the year 1910. Holmes, drawing near to his retirement, was then at the peak of his fame. Houdini, twenty years the younger man, had not yet attained the remarkable international recognition that was soon to be his. The first meeting of these two men was by no means cordial, but while they never became intimates, there developed between them a tacit respect born of the recognition that each was the unparalleled master of his craft.

Their encounter and the remarkable events which attended it form one of the most singular cases of my friend's career. Houdini, always secretive concerning the details of his private life, forbade me to write of the matter within his lifetime. Regrettably, I am no longer bound by that constraint. Houdini is dead well before his time, and by a means which I myself might have foreseen.*

*Houdini died on October 31st, 1926, of acute peritonitis resulting from severe blows to the stomach.

I return, then, to the year 1910. I endeavour to fix the year precisely, for I am not insensitive to the complaints of some of my readers regarding my carelessness with dates. This was the year in which George V ascended to the throne; and a time in which, though we did not know it at the time, dark reverberations throughout Europe drew us closer and closer to The Great War.

John H. Watson, M.D.
2 November 1926

· I ·
THE CRIME OF THE CENTURY

"THE CRIME OF THE CENTURY?" asked Sherlock Holmes, stirring at the firecoals with a metal poker. "Are you quite certain, Lestrade? After all, the century is young yet, is it not?" He turned to the inspector, whose face was still flushed with the drama of his pronouncement. "Perhaps, my friend, it would be more prudent to call it the crime of the decade, or possibly the most serious crime yet this year, but one really ought to resist such hyperbole."

"I must caution you not to make light of the situation, Mr. Holmes," said Inspector Lestrade, standing at the bow window. "I did not travel all the way across town merely for your amusement. The case of which I speak has implications which even you cannot begin to grasp. In fact, I am somewhat overstepping my authority in consulting with you at all, but as I just happened to run across Watson here—"

"Indeed." Holmes replaced the poker in the fire-irons stand and turned to face us. He was wearing a sombre grey frock-coat which emphasized his great height and rigid bearing. Holmes was, as I have often recorded, a bit over six feet tall, thin almost to the point of cadaverousness, and possessed of sharp features and an aquiline nose which gave him the appearance of a hawk. Standing there with his back to the fire and his elbows resting on the mantelpiece, it was difficult to say whether he had struck a posture of ease or advertence. "I think it would be best, Lestrade, if you told your story from the beginning. You say that you suspect this young American of a great crime, is this so?"

"It is."

"And what did you say this fellow's name was?"

"Houdini."

"Yes, Houdini. Watson, will you have a look in the index?"

I selected one of the bulging commonplace books from its shelf and began paging through the entires. "H-o-u, is it? Here is the Duke of Holderness, and here—ah yes! Houdini, Harry. Born on March 24, 1874, in Budapest. This is curious, though . . . there is also record of his having been born on April 26 of that same year, in Appleton, Wisconsin."

"Curious indeed!"

"He is an American magician, best known for his remarkable escapes. It is said that he has never failed to free himself from any form of restraint. He is particularly fond of challenging police officials to bind him in official constraints, from which he then releases himself."

I heard a suppressed chuckle near the fireplace.

"Houdini also has an interest in the new flying machines, and has actually made several short flights himself."

Lestrade scoffed. "That's just the sort of thing I'm talking about! What kind of person is it who tampers with unnatural machinery!"

"On the contrary, Lestrade, I'd say our Mr. Houdini shows a keen interest in the advance of science, as well as a highly adventurous spirit. He sounds like a most surprising individual. Is there anything else, Watson?"

"Nothing," I said, replacing the heavy volume.

"I presume then that you have something to add to Watson's description, Lestrade?"

"I do indeed, Mr. Holmes," said the inspector, reaching into his breast pocket for a small notebook. "Let's see . . . where to begin . . . ah, right!" Lestrade jabbed a forefinger into the notebook. "On the day before yesterday, this fellow turns up at the Yard and demands to be locked up in one of our cells! Well, I've been on the force near thirty years now and this is the first time anyone ever volunteered to be locked up. So we looked him over pretty carefully, and he says, 'I want to be locked up so I can escape!' We all got a good laugh out of that, I can tell you. But this young fellow wouldn't give up! He insisted that he'd done the same thing in Germany and France, and he brought out the newspaper clippings to prove it!" Lestrade slapped his notebook against his open palm.

"Well, Mr. Holmes, it's one thing to break out of those tin boxes they have over there, but our British gaols are the finest in the world. If this little American thought he was just going to walk in and walk out, quick as you please, we were only too happy to oblige him. So we took him into the ground floor cell block and put him in a free cage. Frankly, I thought he'd back away when he saw the lock on the door, but he didn't, so we locked him up tight. I promised to come back for him in a few hours, when he'd had enough."

Holmes looked over at the inspector. "And then?"

Lestrade clasped his hands behind his back and looked out of the window. "Thirty minutes later we received a telephone call in the C.I.D. office. It was Houdini. He said he'd made it back to his hotel all right and he just wanted us to know he'd left a surprise in the cell block. Naturally we didn't believe it, but when we got in there we saw that not only had he broken out, but he'd also switched around every prisoner in the entire wing! Seventeen prisoners and not one of them was in his right cell! We had quite a job just—Mr. Holmes! I fail to see what is so amusing in all this!"

"Quite so, Lestrade," said Holmes with a short cough, "forgive me. But still, I don't see that your problem is as grave as you suppose. I'm sure it's simply a question of improving the design of your goal. Perhaps Mr. Houdini could be persuaded to cooperate—"

"My God, Mr. Holmes!" Lestrade cried impatiently. "Do

you really think me such a fool as all that? The cells are nothing! That was only the beginning! But if he can get in and out of our gaol cells he can get in and out of anything! Anything at all! Some of the men even suspect . . . well, they suspect . . ." He paused and looked down at his notebook.

"Yes?"

"It's nothing."

"There, Lestrade, you were on the point of saying something."

Lestrade cast a wary eye at Holmes and then at me. "I don't believe any of it, mind you, but some of the men say that Houdini is a . . . a spirit medium."

"Oh, come!"

Lestrade held out his palms in a gesture of disavowal. "It's not my theory, I assure you, but it has to be taken into account. I've done a bit of research on this fellow and the results are very surprising. Very surprising indeed. Just consider the facts for a moment, Mr. Holmes, and see what you make of them. Every night, on stages all over the world, Houdini allows himself to be tied up, wrapped in chains, nailed into packing crates, and I don't know what all, and he always gets free! Now what does that suggest to you?"

"Great skill and technical proficiency?"

"Perhaps, but don't you find it in the least strange that he never fails? Not once? Can you say the same?" Here Lestrade was referring, rather indelicately I thought, to the theft of the black pearl of the Borgias, an affair which even Holmes had been unable to penetrate. Though he would soon recover the pearl in a case I have recorded elsewhere,* the matter weighed heavily on him at present. I realized then how great was Lestrade's sensitivity over the issue at hand, for he was never one to open old wounds.

---

*For some reason Watson is referring to "The Adventure of the Six Napoleons," a case which occurred years earlier.

Holmes reached into the scuttle and threw a lump of sea coal onto the hearth. "Occasionally my methods fail me," he observed quietly, "but then, I receive no assistance from the other world."

Lestrade looked away quickly. "I didn't mean to give offense, Mr. Holmes, I'm simply asking you to keep an open mind to this thing, as I've done." He flipped through the pages in his book. "Now, there's a group in America that calls itself the Society for Psychic Research. These aren't witch-doctors in this group, they're scientists and doctors, reasonable sorts like you and me. This Society swears up and down that Houdini achieves his effects through psychic means. They say no other explanation is possible."

"And what of Houdini himself? Does he claim to traffic with the spirits?"

"No, he's denied it repeatedly. But don't you see? Even that fits the theory. If he were using special psychic powers to make a living as a magician, he'd have to conceal his gifts in order to protect his livelihood!" Lestrade gave a nervous laugh. "I know that what I'm saying sounds incredible, but two days ago this fellow walked out of one of our tightest cells without turning a hair. No one has ever done it before, and frankly I doubt if anyone will ever do it again. A thing like that sets me thinking maybe we are dealing with . . . well, with the unknown. Now I'm not saying I hold with all of this psychic claptrap, but after Houdini was at the Yard I went down to the Savoy to see one of these performances of his. What do you suppose I saw?"

"Do tell."

"It was astonishing. I've never seen anything like it. During the course of his magic show, Houdini had his workmen construct a solid brick wall on the stage behind him. There was no trickery about it, I'm certain. The wall was put together brick by brick; it was absolutely solid. And he had it positioned so that he couldn't get around it in any way, but somehow he managed to travel from one side to the other, right before my eyes! Right through the wall! Now how could he possibly have done that?"

"He was assisted by elves?"

"According to the Society for Psychic Research, Houdini can only do this trick by reducing his entire body to ectoplasm."

"Ectoplasm?"

"It's the substance of spirit emanations. What ghosts are made of. I know that sounds ridiculous, but how else could a man pass through a solid substance? At least at Scotland Yard there was a door in the cell, but this was a solid brick wall. So naturally when the theft occurred—"

"Theft?" Holmes was instantly alert. "Would this theft be the crime of the century you mentioned earlier?"

"The same. I can't give you the details just yet because the matter is highly confidential and involves certain highly placed individuals. But I'm convinced that the crime can only have been committed by someone who can walk through walls. Mind you, I'm not saying he actually does walk through walls, but he certainly manages to convey that impression. So if you would just come down to the Savoy with me and have a look—"

"Lestrade, this crime—"

The inspector held up his hands. "I'm sorry, I've told you all I can. You are not an official detective, Mr. Holmes, and this matter is absolutely confidential."

"Then I'm afraid I can't help you."

"What!"

Holmes threw another lump of coal onto the fire. "I am clearly out of my depth, Lestrade. Men made of ectoplasm, thefts of such high confidentiality." He shook his head. "No, no. It's too much for me. Watson, would you care to take a stroll in the botanical gardens?"

Lestrade's mouth fell open. "But—but you don't understand! All I'm asking is that you come down to the theatre with me and see this Houdini for yourself! Now where's the harm in that? It's not so much to ask, is it?"

"I'm afraid it is, Inspector," Holmes said evenly. "You are asking me to enter into a criminal investigation with no knowledge of the actual crime. You are asking me to entertain a theory which accommodates men who walk through walls. I am not an official detective, as you have so conscientiously reminded me, but neither am I a haruspex. Should you need my services in matters pertaining to the corporeal, my door will be open. Until then, good day."

Lestrade let out a long sigh and moved towards the door. "It's just as well, I suppose," he said, taking down his hat and ulster. "We were given specific orders not to consult you on this case. I just thought—"

"Orders?" Holmes whirled about, his features drawn tight. "Orders from whom?"

"Why, the government, of course!"

Holmes stiffened. "What branch?"

"The message came from Whitehall. It was unsigned."

A high colour crept into the gaunt cheeks of Sherlock Holmes. "Lestrade," he said, his voice rigid with emotion, "either you are the most devious man at the Yard or you are an unpardonable lummox."

"What—?" The inspector stammered, but Holmes was already gone, running down the steps to Baker Street, blowing two shrill blasts on his cab-whistle.

· II ·

THE ECTOPLASMIC MAN

HOLMES WAS SILENT as our four-wheeler sped towards the Savoy, and Lestrade, to his credit, knew better than to probe for the source of the detective's sudden agitation. For my part, I had observed these fits of pique on several previous occasions, and I knew them to be grounded in a personal, rather than professional, vexation. As Holmes now seemed to have regained his composure, I thought it best not to remark upon the matter, for I knew that if my suspicions were accurate, all would be revealed presently.

And so I passed the journey wondering what sort of man it was who could so readily divest himself of canvas strait-jackets and pass through solid brick walls. In my long association with Holmes we had been concerned in a score of mysteries which, at their outsets, seemed to involve spirit beings. Crime aficionados still remark upon the macabre affair of the earl, the ascot, and the heavy feather, which had been the despair of several well-trained investigators. Only Holmes had been able to prove that flesh-and-blood murderers were responsible, rather than the vengeful revenants originally suspected by Scotland Yard.

Would Holmes be as successful in penetrating the mysteries of Houdini, or had Lestrade at last presented him with a problem which had no logical solution? This was the challenge my companion had unwillingly undertaken that afternoon. In Lestrade's defense I must say I rather doubt that he ever truly believed all this spiritualist commotion about Houdini. He was, rather, a man who dearly loved to have a key for every lock, no matter how unwieldy the keys became.

I had not been to the Savoy theatre since the passing of my beloved wife, Mary. Together we had attended many of the comic operas of Gilbert and Sullivan there, and though she had been gone many years, the association was still a painful one. My mood was certainly not lightened by the appearance of the theatre itself, which was dark and grim. The plush lobby, which I was so accustomed to seeing brightly lit and filled with cheery theatre patrons, now appeared shadowy and hollow. Through the far doors I could see rows of empty seats which seemed to stretch forever, creating an impression of eerie expectation. I am not ordinarily given to flights of fancy, but I imagined that I could feel my wife's presence in that opulent crypt, and I acknowledged to myself that if I were ever to see a spirit, it would very likely be in this place.

"Do you see this?" Lestrade was saying. "Do you see this, Holmes?" He pointed to one of the dozens of theatrical posters which covered the walls of the lobby. "Houdini claims to have no interest in spiritualism, and yet he draws attention to himself with a poster like this! There's more here than meets the eye, I tell you!"

The poster showed an ordinary wooden barrel secured with chains and heavy padlocks. Above it hovered a likeness of Houdini, who had evidently just wafted from the barrel as smoke rises from a chimney. His legs, the illustration plainly showed, were still vaporous. To strengthen this supernatural impression, the young man was shown receiving counsel from a small band of red demons who scurried about his form, while in the background a number of befuddled-looking officials stood scratching their heads. Below the illustration was printed the legend: Houdini!!! The World's Foremost Escape King!!!

"You are absolutely right, Lestrade," said Holmes. "This is conclusive evidence of the man's spirit capacities. What a fool I have been ever to have doubted you! Now as to the details of this crime you mentioned—"

"Enough of that, Mr. Holmes. You'll be able to see for yourself in just a moment. Remember, though, Houdini doesn't yet know that he's a suspect in the crime, so you musn't let on!"

Holmes turned and walked towards the empty theatre. "As of yet I have nothing to let on," he said.

As we gained a view of the stage I could see a group of four workers carrying large packing crates back and forth across the stage. By his resemblance to the poster illustration, I gathered that the man directing the activity was none other than Houdini himself.

Houdini was a small but powerfully built young man. His black, wiry hair was combed out from the centre into two pointed tufts, which combined with the black slashes of his eyebrows to give him a satanic aspect. His every movement was precise and forceful, yet so fluid and full of grace that I was put in mind of the sleek jungle cats I encountered during my Afghan campaigns. He wore a coal-black suit, which contributed to his dramatic appearance, and though he was smaller than any of his workers, he nevertheless insisted on carrying the largest load.

One of Houdini's assistants drew his attention to our arrival. Upon seeing Lestrade, Houdini gave a cry of surprise and set down his burden. He then leapt across the orchestra pit and made his way towards us, skimming across the backs and arms of the theatre seats as if using stepping stones to cross a river. This display of coordination and balance was not mere bravado, but rather the natural course of one whose control over his own body was so complete that such exertions were as natural to him as walking.

"Mr. Lestrade!" cried Houdini as he jumped down into the aisle where we stood. "It's good to see you!" He gave the inspector a jovial slap on the back. "I didn't expect to see you snooping around until this evening's performance! You're not still upset about that gaol break, are you?"

"No, no," said Lestrade quickly, "I only wished to introduce you to these two gentlemen. Sherlock Holmes and Dr. Watson, allow me to present Mr. Harry Houdini."

Upon hearing my friend's name, the young magician was scarcely able to conceal his pleasure. "I am delighted to meet you, sir," he said, grasping Holmes by the hand and shoulder. "I've admired you for years."

"The honour is mine," replied Holmes. "I trust that you have worked out the difficulties with your rope escape?"

"Why yes, I . . . wait a minute, how did you know I was having trouble with a rope escape?" In his surprise at this observation, Houdini quite forgot to take my hand and slap my shoulder. "I've always read about you doing that, but I never thought I'd actually see it! How did you know?"

"Simplicity itself, my dear fellow. There are several chafing wounds on both your wrists. I have seen identical wounds on the wrists of robbery and kidnap victims who had strained against their bonds for many hours. The natural conclusion is that you have spent some hours attempting to free yourself from a similar restraint, and were, perhaps, less successful than you might have hoped."

"Wonderful!" Houdini cried. "What a trick! But I did get out of that rope tie. I was practising on a new kind of knot. Better to work it out in rehearsal than to have it come at me during a performance." He led us towards the stage. "I sure wish Bess were here to meet you, Mr. Holmes." He paused and struck a theatrical pose. "To Harry Houdini," he intoned, "she is always *the* woman."

This brief reference to one of my early Holmes stories*
was clearly intended to flatter the detective. Houdini could

*"A Scandal In Bohemia," which begins, "To Sherlock Holmes she is always *the* woman."

not have known that Holmes seldom remembered anything but the titles of my stories, when he bothered to read them at all, so it meant nothing to him. Instead, Holmes proceeded immediately to the business at hand.

"Tell me, Mr. Houdini, is it true that you are able to reduce your body to ectoplasm?"

The American laughed. "Is that why you came here? No, Mr. Holmes, as I've been trying to tell Lestrade here, my magic has nothing to do with any witches or ghosts."

"Witches and ghosts have nothing to do with it," Lestrade insisted. "I never said that at all. I merely suggested that if you were a spiritualist you would have to hide your abilities from the public. If it became known that you were able to become immaterial, your escapes would cease to be dramatic. Where's the excitement in an escape artist who can walk right through his chains?"

"On the contrary," Houdini replied, "that would be the greatest act ever staged. People would pay ten bucks a head to see a real live ghost. But I am not a ghost, I'm an escape artist."

Lestrade was not satisfied. "You insist that you are not a psychic, but I still feel that no other explanation is possible for what I have seen on this stage."

Houdini bowed deeply. "Thank you very much, Mr. Lestrade. That is the best compliment a magician could receive."

Lestrade turned to Holmes in exasperation. "I get nowhere with him! Do you see why I wanted you to come down here?"

"Actually, I do not," Holmes answered. "I'm sure you'll forgive me, Lestrade, but your failure to comprehend Houdini's mysteries will not cause me to embrace spiritualism. I submit that some more logical explanation has escaped your notice."

"Are you saying I'm thick, Holmes? Or gullible? I'd like

to point out he's not merely pulling rabbits out of a hat; he's walking through solid brick walls!"

"Pray do not grow testy, Lestrade. I did not invite this interview. Nor am I suggesting that you are slow-witted in any way. I merely observe that in this case you are quick to accept the phenomenal where a more strict logician might turn to the somatic. I have no doubt that the same disciplines which govern the science of deduction would lend some insight into the marvels of Mr. Houdini."

"Pardon me, Mr. Lestrade," Houdini broke in with exaggerated formality. "Did I just understand Mr. Holmes to say that my little mysteries would give him no trouble at all?"

"That is more or less what he said."

"Very well," Houdini said. "Let's just see about that." He turned to the stage. "Franz! Come out here!" An enormous bald-headed man appeared from the wings. "Have the boys set up last night's wall." With a nod, the large man withdrew. "Now then, Mr. Holmes," Houdini resumed, "I think that even you will have some difficulty explaining this. Please follow me."

He led us up a small flight of steps which brought us onto the stage. "If this were an ordinary performance, my workmen would construct a wall brick by brick while I did some smaller effects out here. That way the audience can be sure that there's nothing tricky about the wall itself. It's absolutely solid." As he spoke his assistants spread a large red carpet across the back of the stage. Onto it they wheeled a low platform which supported, as Houdini had promised, a brick wall. "Observe: The wall is nine feet high, seven feet across, and two feet deep." He slapped the hard surface with the palm of his hand. "Sturdy. Now please note that the wall is positioned so that the top and sides are visible to the audience. If I attempted to slip around or over the wall, the audience would see me."

As he spoke Houdini's conversational tone vanished and

was replaced by a practised, resonant mode of speech in which each syllable was carefully accented. His voice travelled out to the farthest reaches of the theatre and came swelling back in waves. One seemed to hear it not just with the ears, but with all the senses.

"I have spread this carpet across the stage in order to rule out the possibility of a trapdoor. You will also note that the platform which holds the wall is only three inches high, far too low to permit me to slip under."

The magician stepped back and gazed searchingly into the distance. "This ancient Hindu mystery has not been performed on any stage for more than two centuries. It was originally part of a sacred rite of passage. The village fakir would prove himself worthy by allowing himself to be sealed inside a deep cave from which he would miraculously emerge. I have brought the effect to England directly from Calcutta, where I was admitted to a holy council of elders—"

"Come, come now," said Holmes.

"What is it?" Houdini snapped, his face darkening.

"Surely if you had come directly from Calcutta you would show some effects of the tropical climate? Instead you are as pale as we are! No, I observe that while your clothing is of an American cut, your collar and bootlaces are German. It seems likely that you have just spent some time in that country, as you were there recently enough to require a new collar, and long enough to have need of new bootlaces."

Houdini paused for a moment and then opened his mouth as if to continue the oration, but immediately he thought better of it. Instead he shouted across to his assistant. "Franz! The screens!" The bald giant reappeared carrying two sections of black screen, each hinged vertically at its centre. These were placed on either side of the wall to create an enclosure which shielded a small portion from view.

"Dr. Watson, if you will stand here . . . Lestrade there

. . . and Mr. Holmes over here . . . thank you very much."
He had positioned us so that the wall was seen from every
angle. "Please remember, gentlemen, that I cannot travel
over, under, or around the wall. I am stepping behind the
screen on this side of the wall. If I appear on the far side,
it can only be because I travelled through the wall to get
there."

He stopped to let us absorb his words. "Now then, if you
are ready, gentlemen. I shall count three. When I am
finished counting, a miracle will have occurred. One . . . two
. . . are you ready? . . . *three!*"

From the other side of the barrier I heard Lestrade give
a cry. "He's done it! He's done it again!" He rushed from
behind the wall, dragging Houdini by the arm. The young
magician was slightly ruffled, but otherwise no worse for his
efforts. I confess that I was thoroughly baffled by the feat,
and by the speed and apparent ease with which it was
effected.

Holmes must have read my expression, for he asked,
"What do you make of it, old fellow?"

"I fear I can make nothing of it," I replied.

"Nothing, Watson? You know my methods, apply them!"

I looked carefully at the American. "His hair is disordered, but I daresay mine would be as well if I passed
through a solid wall!"

Houdini smiled broadly and attempted to smooth his
unruly hair. "Well, Mr. Holmes?"

The detective took his cherry-wood pipe from his pocket
and carefully began to fill it. "Watson, you and Lestrade
have often heard me assert that when one has eliminated all
that is impossible, whatever remains, however improbable,
must be the truth."

"Exactly, Holmes," Lestrade said eagerly. "Houdini has
shown that he could not get around the wall in any way.
Therefore, he must have passed directly through it!"

"I'm afraid that, too, must be eliminated as impossible."

Holmes lit his pipe and sent up a cloud of white smoke. "And if Houdini had travelled over, or to either side of the wall, we would have seen him."

"Well, he can't very well have gone under it, Holmes. Even if there were some sort of opening in the platform, there are only three inches between the wall and the stage!"

"And," Houdini could not help but remind us, "I can't have used a trapdoor because this carpet is covering the stage!"

Holmes smiled benignly at him. "Indeed," he said, "you are quite right. Any trapdoor would be covered by the carpet. And yet, I am reminded of a most instructive musical phenomenon, that of the common drum." As he spoke, Holmes stepped down into the orchestra pit where a large set of drums stood. "In effect, every drum is but a hollow cylinder tightly covered by a flexible membrane." Holmes reached up through one of the smaller drums and placed his hand beneath the drumhead. "Observe: If a solid plane is placed below the membrane, the drum makes no sound." With his free hand he struck the drum, producing only a dull thud. "But when there is nothing below the surface, the membrane is allowed its natural flexibility." He withdrew his hand and struck the drum again. A loud beat echoed through the theatre. "In the drum, sound is produced. However, the principle has other applications."

Houdini and Lestrade stood transfixed by this singular discourse. While my companion lacked the resonance and peacockery of Houdini, his narration was made all the more compelling by its quiet logic and absolute self-assurance. I could see Houdini growing restless as Holmes continued.

"Now let us turn our attentions to Houdini himself." Holmes, still in the orchestra pit, walked to the edge of the stage and found himself level with our feet. "I note a long scuff along the inside of the left shoe. This mark was not there a moment ago. Perhaps the shoes dislike transforming into ectoplasm?" He stepped back onto the stage and took Houdini's arm as if it were a laboratory specimen. "What do we see here? In Houdini's cuff buttons we find strands of red carpeting. This is extremely significant. From this we may—"

"Enough, Holmes!" Houdini snatched his arm away, his face dark purple. "You are mocking me! You are mocking the Great Houdini! You—you—" Houdini then said something in German which had a distinctly unsavoury sound. By Holmes's expression it was clear that the meaning was not lost on him.

"I see that diplomacy is not among your talents, Mr. Houdini," said Holmes. "Perhaps you had best concentrate on those abilities which you do possess, for ill-temper is often overlooked in an accomplished performer. *'Est quadam prodire tenus, si non datur ultra.'* "*

With this rather obscure quote from Horace, Sherlock Holmes turned and was gone.

---

*"Your powers may reach this far, if not beyond."

· III ·

A CALLER AT BAKER STREET

"SEE WHAT I HAVE BECOME in my old age, Watson," Holmes said as we climbed the steps to our lodgings, "an exposer of magicians! Sherlock Holmes, scourge of the conjuror! I'm afraid I am nearing the end of my usefulness."

"You make too much of the matter, Holmes," I said. "Perhaps this morning's encounter was a disappointment, but I'm sure Lestrade will return with a more—"

"Lestrade! The poor man is worse off than I! He has abandoned his reason! Soon we shall find him engaged in earnest conversation with the pigeons in St. James's Park."

"Holmes, you are exaggerating."

"Possibly, possibly. But it is also possible that I have delayed my retirement for too long. I hear the call of the bees."*

I knew then how truly irritated Holmes had been with the morning's proceedings, for he rarely spoke of abandoning his practice. In earlier days he would have extinguished his frustration with cocaine, the fiendish addiction which had once threatened to check his remarkable career, so it was with some relief that I saw him turn instead to the chemical deal table, where a malodorous experiment awaited him.

He was not long at it, however, before the page brought in a calling card to announce another visitor. "Thank you,

*When Holmes finally did retire he moved to the south of England to spend his declining years as an apiarist.

Billy," said Holmes, taking up the card, "show her up. Perhaps this will lead to a more fruitful investigation, Watson. What do you make of this?"

It was an ordinary lady's calling card, which announced a Miss Beatrice Rahner. "I cannot see that there is anything to be learned, apart from the obvious fact that our caller is an unmarried woman."

"That is precisely what we do not learn. See how worn the card is, and the reverse side is stained. No self-respecting maiden would present such a card, she would have fresh ones printed. No, I suspect we are dealing with a married woman who carries this card as a keepsake, and who for some reason wishes to conceal her married state from us. Now," he walked to the bow window and began drumming his fingers on a pane of glass, "let us see. The cardboard stock and the printing are American, so I think we may hazard a guess that our caller is as well. There is something in the name. . . . " He walked to the mantel and took up his black clay pipe. "Beatrice. Watson, didn't our conjuror friend refer to his wife as 'Bess'? I believe that is a common American contraction of—" He walked over to the door and threw it open. There stood a diminutive dark-haired woman with a timid, almost fearful expression. "Won't you come in, Mrs. Houdini?"

Our visitor gasped and her hand flew to her throat. "How could you possibly—?" she began in a quiet American accent. "Never mind. I have long since given up asking Harry to explain his miracles, why should I expect you to reveal yours? Now I am certain that you are the only man who can help me."

"Pray have a seat and tell us in what way we may assist you. This is my associate, Dr. Watson, before whom you may speak freely." I took her hat and cloak and showed her to a seat by the fire.

Mrs. Houdini looked hesitantly from Holmes to me, as if

uncertain of how to begin. "As you have somehow guessed, I am Bess Houdini. You must forgive my trick, Mr. Holmes. One of the stage hands told me that you and Harry, well, didn't hit it off together, and I was afraid you might refuse to see me."

"You misjudge me."

"Perhaps, but you see, my problem concerns my husband and he would be very angry if he knew that I came to see you."

"You wish to escape from your husband."

A bit of fire appeared in Mrs. Houdini's eyes. "He did not care for you either, Mr. Holmes, but you make light of my problem."

"You wish to do away with him then."

"Do not trifle with me, Mr. Holmes! There is no finer man alive than Harry Houdini! I married him not once but three times over, once before a judge, once before a priest, and once before a rabbi! And I would marry him a dozen more times if it were any measure of my devotion to him!"

Holmes favoured her with one of his rare kindly smiles. "My apologies, Mrs. Houdini. Watson will tell you that I am a bit insensitive where the fair sex is concerned. Please tell us why you have come."

Mrs. Houdini took off her gloves, politely accepted my offer of a cup of tea, and began the following remarkable narrative:

"This afternoon you saw how strong-willed my husband can be. I often fear that his . . . his hardheadedness will be his undoing. He will accept any escape challenge no matter how outrageous. I don't think you can imagine what it is like for a woman to see her husband dive securely manacled into a freezing river, or hang upside-down over a crowded street while freeing himself from a strait-jacket. He says he has to do things that no other performer would even attempt. 'Scare 'em off,' as he says.

"Maybe you can imagine, then, how Harry felt when he received some newspaper clippings about a man named Kleppini who was billing himself as 'The King of All Handcuff Kings,' and who claimed to have defeated Houdini in a public contest. This happened about five years ago. We were appearing in Holland at the time. In those days I performed alongside my husband as his only assistant. He always promised that when he became a success I would no longer have to do so, but in truth I deeply miss the . . . are you listening to me, Mr. Holmes?"

Holmes had stretched himself out on the sofa and was trailing an arm and a leg upon the floor. His eyes were closed and to all outward appearances he seemed to be asleep, but I, who knew his moods so well, knew that he had assumed an attitude of utmost concentration. "I am following you quite closely, Mrs. Houdini," he said. "How did your husband respond to this other escape artist?"

"He was furious. He raged for days. 'Who is this man Kleppini?' he shouted. 'I've never even met the man!' Finally he demanded to be released from his contract so that he could confront Kleppini in person. Harry believes if he allows inferior performers to make a quick reputation off of the Houdini name that his own achievements will become meaningless."

"He travelled to Germany, then?"

"Yes, and he took with him a satchel filled with his very best handcuffs. He calls them his 'Handcuff King Defeaters.' "

"Very good," Holmes murmured.

"When my husband arrived in Dortmund, neither Kleppini nor his agent would agree to meet with him, or entertain any notion of arranging an actual public contest. So, that night Harry attended his rival's performance. After a few of what Harry called 'shoddy rope ties,' Kleppini began telling the audience how he had easily escaped from all of

39

the Great Houdini's restraints, while the simplest pair of handcuffs had held Houdini a helpless prisoner. An old man in the audience stood up and shouted that the story was not true. Kleppini called the old man a liar, saying that he could not possibly know whether it was true or not. The old man rushed to the stage, ripped off his false moustache and beard, and cried, 'I know it is not true because I am Houdini!' "

"Bravo!" shouted Holmes. "That is precisely what I myself would have done. Your husband has proven far more ingenious than I suspected."

Mrs. Houdini flushed at this praise. "Yes, Harry forced his hand. Kleppini could not refuse a challenge made in front of an audience. Instead he claimed that he was not ready to accept another handcuff challenge right then, but that if Houdini would return the following evening a contest would be arranged."

"Was that acceptable to your husband?"

"Indeed it was. That gave Harry time to print up handbills and inform the local newspapers. While Kleppini usually played to half-filled houses, the night of the Houdini challenge was sure to pack them to the rafters." Mrs. Houdini took a sip of her tea.

"Several hours before the challenge was to take place, Harry received a visit from Kleppini's manager, a Herr Reutter."

"Indeed," Holmes chuckled. "Indeed!"

"Reutter wished to see the handcuffs which would be used to test Kleppini. Harry showed him the bag of 'defeaters' and explained that Kleppini would be allowed his choice. Reutter picked out a very unusual pair of French Letter cuffs. These were handcuffs which did not lock with a key, but instead were opened by turning the letters on five small cylinders to form a word. Naturally, Reutter wanted to know what word opened the cuffs."

"Surely your husband did not tell him!" I could not help blurting out.

"Dr. Watson," she answered quietly, "my husband is a shrewd man. This, too, was part of his scheme. After swearing Reutter to secrecy, Harry turned the cylinders to form the word *clefs,* the French word for *keys.* The cuffs sprang open. This seemed to satisfy Reutter, who then left after promising once more not to reveal anything to Kleppini.

"As Harry had hoped, the theatre was filled to its capacity that evening. Kleppini began with his usual magic routines, but the audience was impatient for the Houdini challenge to begin. When the time came for the contest, Houdini stepped up to the stage and was greeted by boos and jeers from the audience. You must understand that the Germans are an extremely patriotic people. To them, it seemed that one of their fellow countrymen was being harrassed by a brash, insolent American. My husband, however, speaks fluent German."

"So I have observed," Holmes said dryly.

"So you have, and I am sorry about that. But in this instance Harry put it to better use. Addressing the audience in their own language, he was able to make them see that Kleppini had wronged him. Harry is a brilliant showman, and he very quickly won their favour.

"The time came for Kleppini to select the handcuffs to be used in the test. Of course, Harry was not surprised when the French Letter cuffs were chosen. Kleppini took the cuffs and dashed into a curtained enclosure that had been erected on the stage. Evidently he was checking to be sure that he could open the cuffs. When he emerged he announced that he would accept the challenge. 'I shall escape in minutes!' he claimed. 'And afterwards I shall allow my wife to escape from the Great Houdini's handcuffs! Then we will have shown this American that it is we Germans who lead the world!'

"At this point a fight broke out between Kleppini and my husband. It was several minutes before they stopped pushing each other and shouting horrible insults. But at last Kleppini allowed himself to be handcuffed. He then withdrew to his cabinet enclosure and set to work."

At this crucial juncture in her story, Mrs. Houdini paused and began tugging distractedly at her lace sleeves. It was plain to me that her husband was not the only Houdini with a sense of the dramatic. "Well?" I asked. "What happened then?"

She smiled very pleasantly at me. "After an hour, Kleppini's cabinet was moved aside so that another act could go on. After two hours most of the audience had gone home. Four hours after Kleppini had entered his cabinet, he gave up and begged to be released from the handcuffs. In the presence of a newspaper reporter, Harry spun the cylinders to open the cuffs. *Clefs* was no longer the key word. During their fight on the stage, Harry had changed the letters to F-R-A-U-D."

I have seldom heard Holmes laugh as loudly as he did upon hearing this. While he soon recovered himself, I was left gasping and dabbing at my eyes with a handkerchief. Mrs. Houdini, obviously delighted with the effect of her tale, smiled demurely and took another sip of tea.

"Really, Mrs. Houdini," Holmes said after a moment, "though your story is a charming one, I fail to see how it concerns either Dr. Watson or myself."

"That is what I am just coming to now," she said, setting down her cup and saucer. "You must understand that all of this took place five years ago, and we have heard little of Kleppini since. Occasionally we have had reports that he still claims to have bested the Great Houdini, but in general he is regarded as a buffoon, and he obtains only the very worst bookings. So we did not think much about him until this morning when we received a very mysterious note in the first post."

42

"A note?" Holmes sat up and leaned forward. "What did it say?"

"Only this, Mr. Holmes, 'Tonight who the fraud is we shall see.' "

Holmes walked to the mantel and began refilling his black clay. "Was that the exact wording?"

"Yes."

"Do you have the note with you?"

"I'm afraid Harry would not let me have it. He insisted that there was no cause for worry, and did not wish me to concern myself with it."

"A pity. We might have learned a great deal from the note itself. You suspect this cryptic message came from Kleppini?"

"The word *fraud* led me to believe so."

"Quite. And the peculiar construction of the sentence suggests that the author is not a native speaker of English. You believe this message is a threat of some sort, not merely another escape challenge?"

"What would be the point of another challenge? Houdini has been challenged dozens of times, and he always wins. The man has no equal. Surely Kleppini, of all people, knows that by now."

"But why threaten him? And why now?"

"For the humiliation. For the damage done to Kleppini's reputation and career. Have you never run across a grudge before, Mr. Holmes?"

Sherlock Holmes stood at the mantel staring down at the black and white ivory box which had been a gift from the murderous Culverton Smith. Had he ever opened its lid, Holmes himself would have fallen victim to a grudge of some twenty years' duration, for the box contained a sharp coiled spring dipped in bacterial poison.*

"It sounds to me more like a gesture of frustration than

*As told in "The Adventure of the Dying Detective."

43

a legitimate threat," said Holmes. "At any rate, I don't see what steps we can reasonably take. We can't very well confront Kleppini on the strength of your conjectures."

"That is not what I am asking. I want you and Dr. Watson to come to the theatre tonight and be alert for any trouble. It would be only too easy for some sort of accident to befall my husband during one of his performances. By their very nature, his feats involve danger. If anything went wrong, for any reason, my husband could be seriously injured." She drew in her breath. "Or worse."

"Really, Mrs. Houdini. I am a detective, not a praetorian."

"A what?"

"A bodyguard. You have brought me nothing but suppositions and yet you expect me to dash off to meet this perceived, very likely imagined danger. It is like something in one of Watson's tales, all bluster and no substance."

Mrs. Houdini's face grew ashen. "Is this the legendary Sherlock Holmes? I can't believe it! You are refusing to act because of your personal dislike for Harry, or some . . . some deeper prejudice. I had hoped that you would be above such behaviour." She walked briskly across the room and snatched up her hat and cloak. "I can see that I have wasted my time here. If anything happens to my husband it will be upon your head, Mr. Holmes. Good day to you both, gentlemen." With these words, Beatrice Rahner Houdini turned her back on us and left the room.

Holmes and I sat for some time without speaking. The longer I considered Mrs. Houdini's tale, the more I became convinced that her fears were valid. "Holmes," I said at last, "why are you so unwilling to act? How can you be so certain that there is no danger to the man?"

Holmes said nothing.

"I cannot share your complaisance," I continued. "I trust that you will not mind if I attend the theatre tonight?"

Holmes reached across for his violin. Placing it carelessly upon his knee, he began scratching out a peculiar and haunting melody.

"Holmes, you are insufferable!" I cried. "Houdini's life is in danger!"

Still he said nothing.

As I left for the theatre two hours later, he was still playing the same haunting tune.

· IV ·

HOUDINI PERFORMS

THE SAVOY THEATRE, alive for the evening's performance, had regained some of its remembered grandeur; but my mind was too clouded with apprehension to take any note of the more congenial atmosphere. Surely this Kleppini fellow intended some harm to Houdini, but how would I detect it, much less prevent it? These and other concerns worried at me until a familiar voice broke into my befuddlement.

"Watson! You seem in a daze, old boy! Or are you simply avoiding an old friend?"

It was Thurston, with whom I often shot billiards at my club. Recently he had led me into some poor investments, and we had been seeing less of each other. But as he was accompanied by his wife, whom I had never met, I was obliged to exchange pleasantries with them.

"Come to see the talk of all London, eh Watson?"

"Well, yes I—"

"He's quite a showman, this Houdini. Two days ago I saw him nailed up in a packing crate and dropped into the Thames. He was out in no time. Should have heard the crowd cheer; you'd think he'd walked on water!"

"Indeed, I've been—"

"And he's quite attractive, for an American," said Thurston's wife, who was far from the most prepossessing woman in the room.

"In fact I've—"

"Yes indeed, we're in for quite an evening. Quite an evening."

The conversation ran in this vein for several minutes until the first bell signalled us to take our seats. Mine commanded an excellent view of the stage, but as I peered about, alert for anything that seemed amiss, I feared that if disaster lurked onstage I should be too late to avert it.

The orchestra struck up a bright tune, and Houdini strode briskly into the footlights. "Ladies and gentlemen," he said, spreading his arms to the audience, "often we magicians are accused of having tricks up our sleeves. Let me put a stop to that right now, *like this!*" He tore the sleeves right off his evening jacket and threw them into the front row. From that moment his spell over the audience was unbroken.

What was it that was so enchanting about this man? These many years later, I still cannot be certain. He had about him a kind of valour which issued from attributes well beyond being able to release himself from ropes and chains. I fear Holmes was right to accuse me of tinging these chronicles with romanticism; but there was something in Harry Houdini's eyes, something in the knowing wink he would give to the audience as he faced a new challenge, trammelled in steel and leather. He seemed to be saying, "We'll do this together, right?" And when, after many tense moments, he would at last emerge, wrung with perspiration, clothes torn and hands bleeding, there was indeed a sense of having shared in an immeasurable triumph.

The first part of the evening passed quickly as he moved through a series of escapes and challenges, each more baffling than the last, until he came to what I took to be the climax of the first act.

"My friends," said Houdini, as the heavy maroon curtain lowered behind him, "at this point in my programme I

47

usually exhibit my legendary Walking-Through-a-Brick-Wall illusion. Tonight, however, I will present you with an even more remarkable feat. Ladies and gentlemen, for the first time on any stage, Harry Houdini's Water Torture Cell!"

An ominous tune rose from the orchestra pit as the curtain lifted to reveal a tall glass cabinet filled to the top with water. It was very stark in its construction. While some attempt had been made to suggest oriental scrollwork about its base, the cabinet was in effect four planes of glass joined at the corners by solid wood struts, a design so simple as to preclude any possible gimmickery.

"Before I can proceed with this escape," Houdini announced, "I require the assistance of a volunteer from the audience." He stepped to the edge of the stage and peered out over the audience. "I see that we have a distinguished visitor with us this evening, the author of the amusing Sherlock Holmes mystery tales. Would you be so kind, Dr. Watson?"

I never would have guessed that my readers would respond so enthusiastically to my presence, but as I rose from my seat there came a rousing cheer and a tumultuous round of applause. I blush to recall that I behaved rather foolishly in the face of this demonstration. I stood at my place for some time with tears in my eyes, nodding my head and trying to communicate my gratitude.

"Come along, Doctor," Houdini prodded. "I believe you know the way." Once again I climbed the steps to the stage. "Dr. Watson," said Houdini, leading me to the glass cabinet, "please examine the Water Torture Cell. Do you detect any false bottom or sliding panel through which I might escape?"

I shook my head.

"The panels are solid glass? The wood solid oak?"

I nodded.

"Thank you. Now please have a look at these foot mana-cles. My feet will be locked into these wooden stocks and I will be lowered, head first, into the Water Torture Cell. The foot stocks will then be padlocked to the top of the cabinet and I will be helplessly suspended in the water. Have I explained this clearly? Have I made it"—he winked at the audience—"elementary?"

The audience laughed and a fresh wave of applause began, though how that word became so intimately as-sociated with Holmes I do not know.

"Do you see any means by which I might free myself from the cabinet, Doctor?"

I shook my head once more.

"Would you care to try the escape yourself?"

I shook my head more vigorously, producing yet another wave of laughter.

"Thank you, Dr. Watson. It is time now for the test to begin." Two assistants came forward and fastened the heavy stocks to Houdini's ankles. "For good measure," said he, "I shall also wear these handcuffs. It is infinitely harder to escape from handcuffs when one is underwater. That, however, will be the least of my problems. Doctor, you and the audience may keep track of my progress by means of the large clock you see here. Gentlemen!"

A rope was attached to the foot stocks. Houdini was then hoisted up by the feet and dangled like a fish over the open cabinet of water.

"This ancient Hindu mystery," Houdini proclaimed from his unusual vantage, "has not been performed on any stage for more than two centuries. I have brought the effect to England directly from Calcutta, where I was admitted to a holy council of elders that I might learn the treasured se-cret, or perish in the attempt! Ladies and gentlemen!" he shouted, "I present the death-defying Water Torture Cell!"

The rope was cut and Houdini plunged head first into the cabinet. Water spilled onto the stage as his assistants fastened the heavy stocks to the top of the cell, sealing Houdini within.

For thirty seconds Houdini merely hung suspended upside-down without acknowledging his predicament in any way. Then, quite suddenly, he began to squirm and twist as if trying to draw his manacled hands up to his feet.

A minute passed and I began to wonder how much longer Houdini could remain underwater, when, with a convulsive effort, he managed to free his hands from the manacles. The audience cheered as the open handcuffs drifted to the bottom of the tank, but it still remained for Houdini to free himself from the foot stocks and effect an escape from the cell.

It seemed like hours, but the large clock showed only two minutes when Houdini renewed his struggle. I knew that even a man of his extraordinary physical stamina could exert himself for only so long without oxygen. How much longer could he survive? Could this be the danger Mrs. Houdini feared? I clenched my fists and waited.

Three minutes after entering the tank, Houdini's actions began to grow feeble and desperate. "Free him, Watson!" shouted a voice from the audience. I looked to Houdini's assistants. They were aware of the dilemma, but made no move to aid him. My heart pounded in my throat as I realized that Houdini's life was in my hands.

Four minutes had passed. Houdini began to pound on the glass. By now the audience was in a frenzy. Men shouted, women screamed, and onstage the assistants darted about, whispering to one another, preparing to act. I feared that they would be too late. Houdini expelled a large cloud of bubbles and hung limp in the tank. Looking about for a heavy object, I chanced to see, leaning forward from one of the upper boxes, the face of Bess Houdini. In that face I beheld such a convulsion of terror that I was propelled, quite unthinkingly, into sudden and precipitous action.

Dashing to the wings I seized a fire axe. Franz, the impassive giant, attempted to restrain me, but I broke free, rushed back onstage, and smashed open the cabinet. Water and glass flooded across the stage and into the orchestra pit. Houdini was barely conscious as Franz cut through the heavy manacles and lifted him to the stage.

"Get a doctor!" someone shouted.

"I am a doctor," I replied. "Stand back! Give him room!"

Houdini raised his head and gestured weakly to the wings. "L-lower the curtain," he gasped, his eyes closing.

Though I did not have my medical bag with me, I began to minister to Houdini as best I could. How could I have allowed this to happen? It was plain that the cell had been altered in some way, and now Houdini was on the brink of death. If I lost him, I thought grimly, I would not rest until I had discovered the agent of this outrage, with or without the aid of Sherlock Holmes.

· V ·

AN ASTONISHING RECOVERY

MY BOLD RESOLVES did not carry me very far, for no sooner was the curtain rung down than Houdini, miraculously recovered, leapt to his feet and seized me roughly by the lapels.

"Damn you, Watson," he hissed, "Did Holmes put you up to this?"

"Mr. Houdini," I stammered, "I thought you were in peril!"

" 'In peril?' In dire need of the trusty Dr. Watson? I've done this escape hundreds of times, you idiot! The drowning business is part of the act!" He turned to the shattered glass cabinet and ran an exasperated hand through his wet hair. "Look at the Torture Cell! Who's going to pay for this?"

Franz handed the magician a towel. "Your instructions, Mr. Houdini?"

"We milk it. Wait five minutes, I stumble out looking weak. We leave the broken Torture Cell onstage for the rest of the show. Tomorrow's papers will read: Houdini show goes on despite near tragedy."

"Very good, sir. I'll clear this glass."

"Your wife," I said, falteringly, "she was terrified. I truly believed that you were drowning."

"Bess always looks like that when I do the dangerous stuff. Get out of the way, Watson. Franz! We'll go to Mummy's Asrah; I'll warm them with Needles and Thread.

Charlie! Bring down the house lights. Signal the orchestra. Raise the—Lestrade, what are you doing here?"

In the midst of all this confusion, Inspector Lestrade had stepped boldly from the wings, followed by three large uniformed constables. "I wouldn't raise that curtain if I were you, Mr. Houdini," he said.

"Charlie! Get this buffoon off the stage!" Houdini shouted, as if issuing another stage direction. "Take Watson too!"

"Mr. Houdini!" cried Lestrade, puffing himself up. "You are addressing an officer of the law! Now, it is my duty to inform you that you are under arrest!"

"Yes, yes," said Houdini, "I'm sure that's very interesting, but I have a show to put on. We'll discuss it later."

"We'll discuss it now," said the inspector, placing a firm hand around Houdini's arm. "You are hereby charged with crimes against the Crown!"

"Crimes against the Crown! What are you talking about?"

All at once the commotion onstage was stilled, and we could hear the sound of the still-distraught audience through the curtain. Lestrade, suddenly finding himself the centre of a great deal of attention, cleared his throat and withdrew a notebook from his breast pocket. "Let's just be certain of our facts. You are Harry Houdini, the escape artist?"

Houdini, still wet from the Water Torture Cell, did not bother to reply.

Lestrade cleared his throat again. "Right. Last night your performance was attended by a party of government officials, which included His Royal Highness the Prince of Wales?"

"I had that honour."

"And it had been arranged for you to entertain this party at a private reception following the performance?"

"That is correct." Houdini shifted about uncomfortably. Through the curtain we heard the din of the crowd growing louder.

"This reception was held at Gairstowe House, the government residence in Stoke Newington?"

"Is there a point to any of this? I'd like to continue with my performance."

"The point is this, Mr. Houdini: Last night a thief broke into the vault at Gairstowe House and stole an important package of documents, documents which compromise the security of His Majesty's government. We have reason to believe that you are that thief."

"That's absurd!" cried Houdini. "Why that—you can't possibly mean that! Houdini a thief? A spy? You've made a mistake!"

"Scotland Yard does not make mistakes, Mr. Houdini" —Lestrade glanced briefly at me—"at least not in this case. The evidence is conclusive. You must come with me now. You will be held at the Yard until a trial is arranged."

"I will be *held*? In one of your Scotland Yard cells? You must be joking."

"We have made certain provisions," Lestrade informed him. "You won't be able to escape this time. Now come along with us, please."

"But—"

Franz stepped quietly through the knot of assistants and stagehands gathered about Houdini and Lestrade and spoke urgently to his employer. "Sir, you must go on. The audience thinks you've drowned in the Torture Cell. You must do something."

"Mr. Lestrade," said Houdini, "I'm afraid your little spy story will have to continue without me. I have an audience. Let's go, everyone! Mummy's Asrah! Charlie! The house lights! Signal—"

Two of Lestrade's burly constables grasped Houdini by the arms. "No, Mr. Houdini," said the inspector, "not tonight. You will come with me. Now."

"Look, Inspector, don't you understand? They think I've drowned." Houdini spoke as if explaining algebra to a very dull boy. "I must undo Watson's blunder. We can't have the British public thinking the Great Houdini was drowned in that ridiculous Water Torture Cell. Think of my reputation!"

"The British public may think what it likes. I wished to spare you the humiliation of being arrested onstage. We planned to make the arrest during the interval. But if you insist we shall announce to the public that you are being taken on suspicion of crimes against the Crown. Think of your reputation then, eh?"

The colour drained from Houdini's face and he leaned heavily on the arm of Franz, who was still at his side awaiting instruction. News that the sun had been extinguished could not have had a more profound effect. "Franz," he said quietly, "announce . . . announce that the Great Houdini is unable to complete his performance this evening, but that he invites the public to return at his expense. And Franz"—the young American stared significantly at Lestrade—"tell them to watch the newspapers for news of my greatest escape yet."

With a slight smile, the only mirth I ever saw him betray, Franz bowed and stepped through the curtains. As we heard him address the audience in his clipped Germanic tones, Houdini writhed and grimaced as if each word pierced his soul.

"My performance!" he moaned. "My career! All because of some idiotic policeman!"

"Inspector," said one of the uniformed officers, "there's a crowd of newspaper men out by the stage door. They must have gotten wind somehow."

"All right," said Lestrade. "We'll wait until the theatre empties and take him through the front."

"Harry! Harry, what is all this?" Bess Houdini had found her way backstage and was clearly bewildered by what she found there. "Franz just cancelled the show! Are you all right? I thought you really *had* drowned! Who are these men?"

Slowly, painfully, Houdini explained to his wife that he was suspected of espionage and had been arrested. Neither of them seemed to comprehend how this could have happened. "Bess"—Houdini took her small hands in his—"it is the end of my career! After all those years in the dime museums, all those years we waited to strike it big . . . now what's happened? How can this be?"

Bess Houdini cast a withering look at Inspector Lestrade. "You are the man who has charged my husband with this crime?"

Lestrade nodded.

"Do you believe that he is guilty?"

"I do."

"Do you also believe in justice? That every man must be held accountable for his actions?"

"Indeed I do, and there is no higher justice in the world than that of a British jury."

"There is one higher," said Mrs. Houdini, "and I would fear it if I were you, sir. Dr. Watson?"

"Yes, Mrs. Houdini?"

"Was my tale of this morning the prating of a deluded woman? I told you that some ill would befall my husband, and here we are. Where is the great Sherlock Holmes now?"

"I assure you, Mrs. Houdini, if I have anything to say about it, Holmes will devote his full energies to the matter."

"Thank you."

"Wilkins!" Lestrade called to one of his constables. "Escort Mrs. Houdini to her hotel." One of the large officers took Mrs. Houdini's arm and began to lead her off the stage. "Is the theatre empty yet?" Lestrade called to another of his men. "Where is that music coming from?"

"Wait!" cried Mrs. Houdini, turning to her husband. "Harry! It will be all right! I will—" What happened next occurred very suddenly, and with no malice of intent, but as the officer gripped Mrs. Houdini's arm more firmly to hasten her off, the small woman stumbled and fell heavily to the stage. From where Houdini stood it must have looked as if the constable had shoved his wife to the ground, for he gave a cry of rage, pushed Lestrade aside and quickly dispatched Officer Wilkins with a blow across the chin. Another of Lestrade's men spun Houdini about and landed a thudding blow to his abdomen. It was as solid a punch as I have ever seen, but it had no effect whatever on Houdini. He simply winked at the officer, spread his arms, and said, "Would you care to try again?"

It was at this moment that the heavy maroon curtain was raised to reveal that the theatre was now empty, empty but for one figure, dressed in evening clothes, perched on a seat in the centre of the house, playing upon the violin.

· VI ·

THE VIOLINIST SPEAKS

"GOOD EVENING gentlemen and Mrs. Houdini," said Sherlock Holmes, setting down his violin. "I rather thought you'd have to come out this way. Lestrade, I trust you have a good reason for disrupting Mr. Houdini's performance? I was enjoying it immensely."

"Sherlock Holmes," said Lestrade indignantly, "I should have known you'd be close by, what with Watson making a fool of himself onstage here."

"There there, Lestrade. You'll recall that I've been of assistance to you on one or two occasions in the past. And as for Watson, I fear he was rather too swept away by the adoration of his public to take any note of my presence."

"You were here the whole time, Holmes?" I asked sheepishly.

"In the orchestra pit, Watson. Fiddling along with the Savoy's own excellent musicians."

"You've wasted your time then, Mr. Holmes," said Lestrade. "This is an official investigation of the greatest importance. We no longer have room for amateurs, thank you."

Holmes smiled indulgently. "Why not humour me, eh Lestrade?" he said. "I'm getting on in years, you know. Watson, is Mrs. Houdini recovered from her fall?"

"I'm fine, Mr. Holmes," she answered. "I just slipped. Harry can be a bit overly zealous at times."

"So I see. And how is Constable Wilkins?"

"Still unconscious, Holmes," I replied.

"Will be for some time," added Houdini, proudly.

"Very well. Then suppose we take a few moments while Wilkins recovers to review the case against Houdini. You say that he has stolen some documents, Lestrade? Is this your own idea?"

"Our case against Mr. Houdini is quite complete. We have our man."

"And yet you are taking some care in avoiding the gentlemen of the press. You have never been one to avoid taking the credit in a case, Lestrade. In fact, I have often known you to take mine. Can it be that your case is not as secure as you might like us to believe?"

Lestrade was silent.

"Now then, what is the nature of these documents which Mr. Houdini is said to have acquired?"

"I am not empowered to say," Lestrade answered sullenly.

"Meaning that you do not know. Now, correct me where I go astray in these conjectures, but am I safe to assume that there were quite a few people at Gairstowe House last night, or did Houdini and the prince have a tête à tête?"

"It was a rather large party, for all that it matters, including a good number of diplomats and their wives."

"Dear me! Diplomats and their wives, characters quite above reproach! And Houdini was invited along to lend dignity to the occasion?"

"He was asked to perform some conjuring tricks."

"I thought it might be something like that."

"He is said to have greatly amused the prince."

"I was brilliant," said Houdini. "Absolutely brilliant."

"Were you?" asked Holmes, amused by the magician's brashness. "And having wrung that confession out of you, may we also know if you did in fact nip upstairs to steal these mysterious documents?"

59

"Certainly not!"

"His footprints were found in the room, Holmes!" Lestrade said hotly.

"Ah, we begin to hear the facts. Houdini's footprints were found in the room. This will warrant a trip up to Gairstowe House, Watson. Tell me, Lestrade, have you yet had a chance to read my little monograph upon the subject of footprints? No? You might find it instructive. I have found that footprints are generally the most unreliable clues in the entire field of detection. Anything else?"

"Well, as you know, there have been certain measures taken to assure the security of Gairstowe House. The vault is said to be the most impenetrable in England. We know of only two men—"

"And both of them are at Newgate," Holmes mused. "I see. So you drew up a list of others who might possess sufficient skill with locks and found—to your great delight —that one such person was present at the gathering. Not enough to hang a man, Lestrade."

"There was the footprint."

"We return to that, do we? There is an agreeable constancy about you, Inspector."

"See here, Holmes, I have been instructed to make an arrest in this case, and I have done so. The thing is bigger than you suspect. I have been in conference with Secretary O'Neill himself!"

"And you resisted your natural inclination to place him under arrest? Charitable!"

"You are attempting to goad me into revealing what I know. It will not work, Holmes. This is an official investigation now and it must remain so. Has Wilkins come around yet? Good, then let's be off."

"Just one last thing," said Holmes, replacing his violin in its case. "How do you propose to confine Mr. Houdini? Suppose he once again reverts to ectoplasm?"

Lestrade flushed angrily. "All right, Holmes, there's no need to bring that up again. I can see that I was misled. This time when I lock him up, he'll stay locked up. Here Wilkins, why don't you show Mr. Houdini what a proper pair of British darbies looks like?"

The still-dazed officer locked a pair of handcuffs roughly onto Houdini's wrists. The escape artist examined them with disdain. He seemed on the point of banging them against a chair when Holmes stepped over and placed a hand on the manacles.

"I implore you," he said, "do not attempt to escape either from the handcuffs or the prison cell. To do so would be an admission of guilt. You must go along with them."

"But Holmes, these cuffs are child's play! Toys!"

"Nevertheless, you will remain in Lestrade's custody. I shall act on your behalf. You must remain at the Yard"—Holmes parodied the magician's conspiratorial wink—"until I send for you. Agreed?"

We heard a brief jangle of steel, and Harry Houdini extended his free right hand to seal the bargain.

· VII ·
A WEIGHTY MATTER

"HOLMES," I began when we had left the theatre and were walking briskly along the Strand, "what if—"

"My God, Watson!" cried he. "You are as inconstant as a woman!"

"What can you mean, Holmes?"

"You were about to suggest that Houdini might well be guilty of this theft, when only three hours ago you were chastising me for failing to assist him."

"Is it not possible that he is guilty?"

"Possible, of course, but hardly probable. We won't know for certain until we have investigated further at Gairstowe House. But I believe that Mr. Houdini is rather too busy with his chosen career to concern himself with such trifles as the theft of government documents."

"Then you believe this business is the work of Kleppini? And our client has been made to look guilty?"

"Perhaps. Decidedly clumsy job of it, though. Rather like your performance on the stage this evening."

Mercifully, the street was too dark for Holmes to see my face redden. "You cannot fault my actions this evening. As I explained earlier, I truly believed that Houdini was drowning. I've no doubt that you would have acted as I did, had you been onstage."

"I tend to doubt it, good fellow. I have never known a drowning man to have the presence of mind to consult a clock, as Houdini did this evening. You forget that I was in the orchestra pit at the time."

"Yes, indeed. Awfully clever, actually. You didn't even have to wear a disguise. No one would have thought to look for you there."

"Actually, there was one man who thought of it."

"Oh?"

"When I gained permission to play along in the pit, the obliging conductor delivered this message." He handed me a sheet of plain note paper, upon which was written: "Join me after the performance."

"This is impossible!" I ejaculated.* "Who can it be from? Who could have known that you would be in the orchestra?"

"Who else?" said Holmes with a shrug. "My brother, Mycroft. He even knew that I would play third chair."

"And it was he who forbade Lestrade to give you the details of the case?"

"Undoubtedly."

Though all emotions—particularly those as virulent as envy—were abhorrent to my friend's admirably balanced mind, I had often noted in him considerable jealousy whenever his elder brother, Mycroft, was mentioned. "That is where we are going, then? The Diogenes?" But Holmes walked on in silence.

I have recorded elsewhere that the Diogenes was the queerest club in London; a place where no member was permitted to take the slightest notice of any other member. Apart from the Stranger's Room, talking was strictly forbidden in the Diogenes Club, and any member heard speaking aloud was liable to expulsion after three violations of the rule. The club had been established, with Mycroft Holmes as a founding member, to accommodate the most unsociable, unclubbable men in the city.

However peculiar the Diogenes might have been, it was made even more so by the regular presence of Mr. Mycroft

---

*A word that had a wider use and broader meaning in Watson's day.

Holmes. As I had been living with Sherlock Holmes for some years before he ever mentioned having a family at all, I was fairly taken aback to discover not only the existence of a brother, but a brother possessed of an even keener mind than that of Sherlock Holmes himself.

"If the art of detection were confined to the armchair," Holmes had once remarked, "my brother would be the greatest criminal agent who ever lived. But he abhors any kind of activity, save cerebral. He would rather be thought incorrect than take the trouble to prove his conclusions."

And so the talents of Mycroft Holmes were unknown but for a select circle of government officials who depended upon them. While he had come to government service as an office clerk, Mycroft's gifts soon made an indelible impression upon Whitehall. He became a clearing-house of information. All the various branches of service would feed their conclusions directly to him; for only Mycroft, in an administration crippled by specialization, possessed the breadth and mental agility to make truly comprehensive decisions. The machinations of his splendid mind became so central that it was said, on occasion, Mycroft Holmes *was* the government. Thus, I should have understood that if the Houdini matter involved the government, by definition it involved Mycroft. Was it any wonder, then, that at times even Sherlock Holmes was awed by this staggering intellect?

"We have not seen Mycroft for some time," I wondered aloud. "What can he have been doing in all that time?"

"Perhaps you would prefer to attach yourself to Mycroft for a time, eh Watson?" Holmes said curtly. "You may be growing weary of my poor exploits."

"I shall never grow weary of your exploits or your companionship," I replied. "And besides, in order to observe Mycroft one would have to become as sedentary as he. That would hardly suit an old campaigner like myself." In the guttering light of a streetlamp I saw Holmes smile to himself.

Our walk took us through one of London's most unsalubrious neighborhoods and, at last, into the more agreeable setting of the Diogenes. We were admitted by the deaf-mute butler and shown into the Stranger's Room, where Mycroft Holmes stood in wait for us. Though he was careless in many aspects of social custom, Mycroft made it a point to be standing whenever he received visitors. It occurs to me now that he did so to avoid being seen struggling from his chair, for Mycroft Holmes was corpulent to an astonishing degree, and for him the simplest movements required considerable and often awkward exertion.

"Sherlock!" he cried with unaccustomed geniality. "Good of you to come. Will you take some port with me? And Doctor"—he gave my hand a fleshy press—"I am delighted to see you again as well. I must say, though, that I have noticed two or three split infinitives in your recent chronicles of my brother's doings. Careless, Doctor. Careless!"

"Mycroft," said Sherlock Holmes, failing to respond to his brother's conviviality, "we have not seen one another in three and one half years. Surely you did not call us over at this hour to discuss Watson's literary shortcomings?"

Mycroft sighed and lowered himself, with great effort, onto a settee. Though all physical resemblance to his brother was distorted by his massive bulk, his features retained some of the same sharpness of expression, and his eyes seemed always to hold that introspective look which I had observed in Sherlock's when he was exerting his powers to their fullest. It was that cast which spread over Mycroft's face now, replacing the laboured joviality of his greeting, as he lapsed into the peculiar telegraphic dialogue which the two brothers favoured when addressing each other.

"You are looking into the matter?"

Sherlock nodded. "And you?"

"Enormous complications."

"So I gather."

"Do not insist."

"My client—"

"A bad business."

"Houdini is innocent."

"Perhaps."

"Most likely."

"Even so."

"Must he be detained?"

"Diplomatic appeasement."

"How so?"

"The German business."

"And Houdini?"

"Footprint."

"Tut!"

"Is German."

"Hungarian."

"Allied."

"Come." As always, the full import of their exchange lay in what was left unsaid, but it was obvious even to me that Mycroft was withholding information crucial to us.

"His father was a murderer," said Mycroft.

"Indeed?" Sherlock raised an eyebrow. "That is the sort of shabby reasoning I expect from Lestrade. One may never judge the son by the father's example, as we have good cause to know."

Mycroft gave a start and opened his mouth as if to reply, but he remembered my presence and decided against it. Here in the Stranger's Room I would catch, on occasion, an unexpected glimpse into the boyhood of Sherlock Holmes; but these images were so slight and so fragmented, like a reflection upon water, that I have never been able to piece them together into any manner of sense.

"I hardly think that . . . we are dealing in an entirely different matter here," said Mycroft, fitting a cigar into his meerschaum holder.

"And what sort of matter is it, then? What are these stolen documents which are of such interest to the prince, Secretary O'Neill, and Mycroft Holmes?"

"Documents, Sherlock. Very important documents. I see now that I cannot dissuade you from pursuing the affair, and you will no doubt discern most of the germane information within a few days, but you may not know the nature of the documents at its core."

"Then how may I gauge Houdini's possible motivation and involvement in the matter?"

Mycroft gave a short laugh. "That is the very least of my concerns."

"Then it becomes the greatest of mine," said Sherlock Holmes. "Come along, Watson. We shall have a busy day tomorrow."

Mycroft Holmes did not rise to see us out.

· VIII ·

SHERLOCK HOLMES
INVESTIGATES

IN THE WOODED UPPER REACHES of Stoke Newington, four
miles from any other structure, sits the government office
known as Gairstowe House. In all respects it appears to be
an ordinary country estate, but for the two-storey row of
offices jutting from its left wing. This oddly shaped building
is surrounded by a tall wrought-iron fence, at the entrance
of which stands a uniformed guard. On the morning following our episode at the Diogenes, the guard on duty was
named Ian Turks. Upon our arrival at Gairstowe, I found
myself making this young man's acquaintance while
Holmes immediately threw himself down on all fours and
began crawling about the grounds of the estate.

I have no doubt that Turks had never before seen a well
turned-out, middle-aged gentleman behave in such a manner. Holmes sniffed about like a bloodhound, examining
patches of grass with his convex lens and occasionally lying
prostrate for several moments at a time, evidently absorbed
in the deepest concentration. Though Turks, like the Palace Guards, was obviously trained to remain impassive in
unusual situations, at length the young man was unable to
contain his curiosity.

"Pardon me asking, mate," said he, "but what is that
fellow doing on the ground there?"

"Looking for footprints, no doubt," I answered.

"Footprints! But all the footprints are inside! The bob-
bies found 'em."

"He is aware of that, but he tends to carry his examinations a step or two beyond those of the official detectives."

"Who is he, then?"

"Mr. Sherlock Holmes."

Turks gave a low whistle and stared again at my companion, who had now rolled over on his back to survey the soles of his own shoes. "That's who he is? Cor! He's better looking in the drawings, isn't he!"*

Before I could formulate a reply, Holmes leapt to his feet and shouted across the grass to me. "Come along, Watson! There is nothing more to be learned here!"

Together we climbed the marble steps which led into the large entrance hall. There our cards were taken by a butler —rather too formally dressed for the early hour—who returned in a moment to conduct us into the presence of Lord O'Neill, the Secretary for European Affairs.

We were shown through a narrow corridor hung with oriental tapestries and into a large study lined with oak bookcases. Behind a scrivener's desk sat the man whom I took to be Lord O'Neill, and across from him sat a very large gentleman of stiff bearing, whom I did not recognize.

"Sherlock Holmes!" cried Lord O'Neill, rising so hastily that he swept a small stack of papers onto the floor. "I was delighted to receive your wire this morning! I had wanted to send for you myself, but your brother, Mycroft, he, well —" He trailed off nervously. "And you must be Dr. Watson! You are welcome here, sir. Ah! Forgive me! I have been remiss! Allow me to present the honourable Herr Nichlaus Osey of Germany."

The German rose and bowed formally in our direction. "I am pleased to meet the famous crime specialist," he said in well-practiced English, "though I did not expect that you

---

*The Holmes stories were originally illustrated for *The Strand Magazine* by Sidney Paget, who drew from a model considerably handsomer than Holmes.

would look quite this way," he added, looking askance at Holmes's dishevelled, grass-stained clothing.

"Mr. Holmes's methods are a bit unorthodox," Lord O'Neill said quickly, "but his results speak for themselves I assure you, I assure you. I was telling Herr Osey of your invaluable assistance during that ugly business back in 1900."

"Ah, yes," said Holmes carelessly, "a simple case, but not without some features of interest. I have recorded it in my notes as 'The Adventure of the Discursive Italian.' "

"Holmes," I asked, though I saw that Lord O'Neill was anxious to proceed, "do you mean to say that you keep your own records of your cases?"

"Don't look so hurt, old fellow! At the time you had deserted me for Mrs. Watson. I could not allow your lapse to disrupt the flow of crime history."

"Fascinating," I said. "May I—?"

"Gentlemen, please!" Lord O'Neill cried. "The affair before us is a most pressing one! We must attend to it. Shall I ring for tea? Yes, we must have tea." He darted to the bell-rope and pulled it urgently.

"Tea!" exclaimed Herr Osey. "At such a time! And all of this talk about records and discursive Italians. It is a wonder you British ever accomplish anything!"

"Herr Osey, please," said Lord O'Neill anxiously. "I'm sure—"

"Who is this remarkable woman with whom the prince has been so indiscreet?"

Many times in my years with Holmes have I seen him produce a startling revelation from the midst of seemingly unexceptional circumstances, but never has one of these abrupt observations had such tremendous impact. It was as if the two diplomats had been struck by lightning.

"Mr. Holmes!" cried Lord O'Neill, leaping to his feet.

"Mein Gott!" shouted Herr Osey. "Can this be? How could you—"

"Your tea, sir," announced the butler, rolling in a large tea-trolley.

Herr Osey thrust his fists into his pockets and turned to the wall. Lord O'Neill fell heavily into his chair, the colour draining from his face, but he managed to collect himself sufficiently to acknowledge the arrival of the tea. The butler then withdrew, and both men turned to stare at Sherlock Holmes.

"Gentlemen! It is perfectly obvious! Allow me to explain. Lestrade has been good enough to leave the room in order, so it is not difficult to see that a conference of some sort took place here on the night of the crime. The brandy snifters on the sideboard point to a late evening, very likely while the larger gathering was taking place downstairs. The desk calendar has not been advanced since the day before yesterday. As Lord O'Neill is rather fastidious in such details, we may assume that the room has not been in use since then."

"Perfectly sound," admitted Lord O'Neill. "But how—"

"That the conference was an important one is rather strongly suggested by the presence of the Prince of Wales. Here is a cigar stub bearing the mark of his private stock. Even more revealing are the contents of this ashtray beside the armchair. In it there are two cigarette ends stained red. Unless one of you two gentlemen has taken to painting his lips, we may infer the presence of a woman.

"What sort of woman is it who smokes in such company? A rather strong-willed woman, certainly. Also, it would seem, a familiar of the prince. Yet, rather than make use of the cigarette case we see here upon the desk, this woman's cigarettes were provided for her by Herr Osey, whose own stubs we see here in the same ashtray. This fact is not without implication."

Herr Osey took the cigarette from his lips and stamped it out peevishly.

"The woman is a German, involved in some sort of diplomatic unpleasantness. This much is obvious by the involvement of you two gentlemen. So, what is the scene we have evolved? A large gathering at Gairstowe House after the theatre. While they are being entertained downstairs, a smaller party assembles in this room to discuss business. This business must concern the documents which have since vanished. The prince and this mysterious woman"—Holmes paused and looked to Herr Osey.

"The Countess Valenka," the German provided.

Holmes nodded. "—would not customarily be present at such an interview. Therefore they are the principals and you gentlemen are their representatives.

"What can be the unpleasantness which would induce two former intimates to employ diplomatic representation? Well, now. The prince has certain . . . compromising tendencies which are well known. Perhaps he has placed himself in the awkward—"

"Mr. Holmes, please!" cried Lord O'Neill wildly. "We have followed your reasoning quite closely. Pray do not continue!" While Herry Osey had listened to Holmes's discourse with a fascinated detachment, Lord O'Neill had become increasingly anxious, and he was now unable to control himself. "You have perceived the nature of our difficulty, and can now appreciate that it is sensitive beyond my ability to speculate."

"Letters, then?"

"Letters," confirmed Herr Osey.

"Confound it! There is no milk for this tea!"

"No matter, my friend," said Herr Osey. "We shall take it dark."

"Yes, quite right," said Lord O'Neill with an embarrassed laugh. "It's a silly thing, I know, but my nerves—"

"Indeed. We are all on edge." Herr Osey took a cup of tea. "It is as you say, Mr. Holmes. We had met to discuss a number of indiscreet letters of which the countess was threatening to make use."

"And it is these letters which are now missing?"

"Yes," Lord O'Neill resumed. "She had turned them over to us, after much discussion and a promise of rather substantial remuneration. But when I returned the following morning, the letters were missing."

"Did you examine the room thoroughly? Was it disturbed in any way?"

"Nothing was disturbed or missing save the letters. And the only evidence of an intruder was these footprints behind the desk."

"The footprints! Of course, let us have a look at the footprints," said Holmes, crawling behind the desk. "Hmm. Most remarkable. Watson, would you step over here?" he asked, brandishing his convex lens. "Have a look, will you?"

Behind the desk was a muddy cluster of footprints which seemed to have been made by someone shuffling in place for a time. "We are told that these are the footprints of Mr. Houdini," Lord O'Neill said.

"Quite right!" Holmes agreed. "In fact, I've had occasion to examine his shoes recently and I recognize the tread. And yet, I must say that in all my years of practice I have never seen such unusual impressions."

"What is so extraordinary about them, Holmes?" I asked.

"What? My good fellow, what about them is ordinary? Observe: In an ordinary footprint the greatest pressure is exerted by the heel and ball of the foot. In these impressions, the greatest weight has been placed on the direct centre of the foot, the arch. What does this suggest to you?"

"Wooden legs?"

Holmes turned to me with a look of surprise. "You never cease to amaze, Watson," he murmured. "Indeed, one wooden appendage is possible, but two? I think it more likely that these prints were made by a hand bearing down on the centre of a shoe."

"In order to implicate Houdini?"

"Obviously. But what is truly suspicious is that there are no footprints leading to or away from this cluster. Could our muddy-footed thief simply have appeared directly in the centre of the room? And as to the mud itself, that is indeed peculiar. You are aware, Watson, that I have made a little study of the varieties of mud to be found about London. It is a useful knowledge for tracing one's movements by the spots upon his trouser cuff. Yet I cannot place the origin of this mud."

"Why, it is the mud from outside, surely," volunteered Herr Osey.

"Surely. But where outside? Not on the grounds of this estate. Of that I am certain. When we have located the source of this mud we shall have gone a long way towards our solution, I assure you." Holmes stood up and gazed vaguely about the room. "It was just the four of you, then?"

"Yes."

"No one else came in or out?"

"Just the serving man."

"Oh?"

"We had tea then, as well."

"At that hour?"

"The prince enjoys it."

"Quite right. I had forgotten. And when your business was concluded, the letters were surrendered and placed in the desk?"

"In this lower drawer."

"Pardon me," I ventured, "but am I to understand that the letters were left in an unlocked drawer? We were told that they were placed in a vault."

Lord O'Neill could not resist chuckling at my confusion. "Dr. Watson, this room *is* a vault."

"I don't understand."

"Let me show you," said Lord O'Neill, leading me into the narrow corridor through which we had entered. "See here," he said, pulling aside the oriental hangings to reveal, recessed into the wall itself, an enormous vault door and the rails upon which it ran.

"Exactly like a bank vault," I said admiringly.

"Actually, my friend, it is considerably more secure," said Lord O'Neill with pride. "There are three separate locking mechanisms contained in this door. One British, one American, and the third European, making this one of the most secure vaults in the Empire. So you see, as there are no other entrances to the room, and no windows through which a man might pass, any object left in this room is as good as in the bank."

"Or so you thought," remarked Herr Osey.

"Yes, or so we thought."

"Well, do not despair," said Holmes. "We have but a few questions and then Dr. Watson and I shall make every effort to bring the matter to a happy conclusion. First, may we assume that no one can leave or enter the grounds of the estate without being observed by the guard?"

"Yes. There is a guard round the clock, and they keep an admitting list."

"May we have a copy of the list for the evening of the reception?"

"I'll have it drawn up immediately."

"Please be certain that it includes any help you were required to lay on for the affair—kitchen staff, footmen, and so on."

"As you wish."

"Fine. Now then, do you have a portrait of the Countess Valenka?"

"No, Mr. Holmes. I do not."

Herr Osey cleared his throat. "This may be of some use,"

he said uneasily. He drew out his pocket-watch and opened it towards us. There on the inner cover was an ivory miniature of one of the most striking profiles I have ever seen.

"The countess gave this to me some time ago," Herr Osey told us. "I realize that a photograph would be of more use to you, but—"

"Not at all, Herr Osey," said Holmes as he bent over the miniature. "True, a photograph would have been more practical for purposes of identification, but this is informative nonetheless." He glanced upward as Herr Osey closed up his watch and replaced it in his waistcoat pocket. "Yes, well. Humph. Where may we call upon the countess?"

"She is staying at the Cleland."

"Very good. We shall be on our way, then. Our first order of business is to exculpate Mr. Houdini, then we shall call upon the Countess Valenka. Good day, gentlemen."

"Mr. Holmes," said Lord O'Neill, "we are considerably less interested in the innocence or guilt of Mr. Houdini than in the recovery of the stolen letters."

"Yes," agreed Herr Osey, "let that be your first consideration."

Sherlock Holmes picked up his hat and stick, and, striding blithely past the vault door, affected not to hear.

· IX ·
HOUDINI BOUND

SHERLOCK HOLMES makes it a point never to discuss a case while it is in progress. I say that this reticence is but vain posturing on his part, satisfying that peculiar love of the dramatic which has made his investigations so notable. Holmes insists that he merely wishes to avoid idle speculation which might bias his conclusions. Whatever the reason, this refusal to deliberate is one of his least endearing fancies, and try as I might as we left Stoke Newington, I could not persuade him to answer any of my questions. Indeed, all the way to Baker Street it seemed that he would talk of nothing but haemoglobin.

"Mark my words, Watson," said he, "we shall soon see police investigators all over the world locked in their laboratories, bent over microscopes to look at haemoglobin. It is inevitable."

"Do you truly believe that bloodstains are more useful to criminologists than, say, footprints?" I asked, attempting to draw him out on the Gairstowe problem.

"Decidedly," he answered. "Once the full properties of haemoglobin are known and understood, the traditional methods of tracing criminals will be abandoned as musty relics. I have known it for years."

"Surely not footprints!" I persisted. "Such as the footprints in Lord O'Neill's study? Won't these footprints be of use to you in this case?"

"Footprints! Footprints are boorish clues, Watson! See

how easily a mind such as Lestrade's is led astray by them! Haemoglobin affords the analytic precision of modern science, whereas a footprint is subject to any number of variants. A footprint may expand or contract, or be trod upon by one of Lestrade's henchmen—"

"But surely the traditional methods of crime detection may be reconciled with the advantages of the laboratory? For example, if you were able to analyze the unusual mud used to make the prints—?"

"No, no, good fellow. That small irregularity would in no way be illuminated in the laboratory. Now, if the thief had been so obliging as to leave a bit of haemoglobin—"

"Holmes! You are insufferable! Will you tell me nothing about the Gairstowe matter?"

"My dear Watson, the facts—such as they are—are all before you."

"But I can make nothing of them."

"Nothing, Watson? Can this be the man whose natural wit and perspicacity are the delight of millions? You have seen all that I have seen, but you have not observed. Think, Watson! Cudgel your brain!"

"Well," I began, endeavouring to employ my friend's celebrated logic, "whoever stole these letters must have known of their existence in advance. This limits our suspects considerably."

"Excellent!" cried Holmes. "Proceed."

"The thief must have been connected with the diplomatic party in some way, to have gained access to Gairstowe House. Either as a guest or an employee."

"You surpass yourself! Pray continue."

"Further," I went on, much pleased with my companion's enthusiasm, "he would have to possess the remarkable ability to penetrate what is, in effect, a bank vault."

"Marvellous!" cried Holmes, applauding vigorously. "You have painted a precise portrait of our suspect. I must say, Watson, that if I find one fault in these chronicles which you occasionally lay before the public, it is that you often flatter me by making yourself appear dim-witted in comparison. You are far too modest concerning your own gifts."

"Why Holmes," I said, deeply moved, "these are kind words indeed!"

"Yes, while it is true that you have taken a somewhat rudimentary view and perceived only that which is painfully obvious, you have nonetheless provided a succinct and functional summary."

"But——"

"Come now, Watson. If we base our speculations on the facts as you have just outlined them, who must our prime suspect be? Who had both the opportunity and the ability?"

"Houdini," I admitted sheepishly.

"Precisely. And what place does Kleppini, who was in no way connected with the gathering at Gairstowe, have in your summary?"

"None," I said.

"Exactly. But do not despair. The matter is quite complicated. I believe that even my brother, Mycroft, has failed to recognize the true depth of this problem. And if we should fail . . ." His voice trailed off.

"Holmes," I persisted, "what if we *should* fail? Suppose the letters were to become public?"

"At best, a dark and protracted scandal. But at a time when succession seems so close, and relations with Germany are so strained——"

"Then we must recover the letters," I said resolutely. "It is not the first time we have averted a royal scandal.* Where shall we begin?"

"We shall begin, stout fellow, by leaving you off at Baker

*In fact, it was at least the fourth time.

Street. There are one or two small points which I must look into on my own."

"But Holmes—"

"It won't do, Watson. This is one of those rare occasions when your presence would be a hindrance."

"But what are you going to do? Will you see the countess?"

"The countess? No, decidedly not, Watson. Not without you. The countess is a woman. I should be foolish indeed to interview a woman without availing myself of your natural gifts." He chuckled merrily to himself. "In fact, I was on the point of suggesting that you pay a call on the countess in my absence."

"Me? What would I say to her?"

"Take her measure, Watson. Uncover her true motives with that quiet, fascinating charm of yours. See if you can't discover what really happened between her and the prince. And more importantly, I must know whether or not she still cares for him. Only then will we know if we are dealing with a blackmailer or a jealous lover."

"All right," I nodded, "I'll go straight away."

"Ah, wait," Holmes said as a new thought struck him, "if I may impose still further upon your good nature, I suggest that you first go to see how Houdini is getting on at the Yard. Remind him of his pledge to remain there. I fancy that by this time he is, shall we say, fit to be tied."

In fact, that expression proved more accurate than Holmes could have imagined, for I arrived at Scotland Yard to find Houdini not only tied, but chained and manacled as well. Evidently, Lestrade had realized that merely confining Houdini in a cell was not sufficient proof against escape. Accordingly, I found Houdini tied to a chair with a length of rope which had been looped about his body so many times as to resemble the shroud of an Egyptian mummy, leaving only his head exposed. Over this cocoon were wound several lengths of steel chain, tightly fastened by several formidable padlocks, and finally, to all this was added several of the heavy leather straps used to restrain madmen. Any of these restraints would have sufficed, so that the layering of them was stifling and uncomfortable, and, in Houdini's case, humiliating.

"Dr. Watson," said the unfortunate man, managing a weak smile, "forgive me if I don't get up."

"Mr. Houdini!" I cried angrily, gripping the small barred window of his cell. "This treatment is outrageous! It is unnecessarily severe! I shall speak to Lestrade at once!"

"Don't bother, Doctor," said Houdini with a bitter laugh, "Bess is with him now. Believe me, if she cannot move him, he has a heart of stone."

"It simply is not decent that you should be treated in this way," I insisted.

"Well, it *is* unnecessary," he sighed listlessly. "I told them I would not escape. Houdini always keeps his word. If I wanted to escape, Dr. Watson, these little annoyances wouldn't stop me."

It was a noble sentiment, and bravely spoken, but Houdini could muster only a trace of his former conviction. Seeing him thus, helpless and dispirited, eyes glazed and expressionless, I was reminded of a bird of prey when its wings are clipped for sport. I should have preferred his customary overweeningness to this, for now, bereft of his fire and dignity, Houdini had become the palest shadow of a man.

At that moment the far door to the cell block was opened and Bess Houdini was shown in by the duty constable. "Harry," she called, rushing over to her husband's cell, "Harry, I have done my best, but that Lestrade is impossible. He insists that you will escape if he lets you up. I told him that you gave your word, but he said that your word meant nothing to him. I gave him a good piece of my mind for that, I can tell you!"

Houdini stared down at the floor.

"Dr. Watson," said the small woman, turning to me, "this business hasn't gotten into any of the newspapers, has it? Harry would be ruined. A performer must guard his reputation offstage as well as on. Any stain or suspicion of misconduct sets everyone whispering. If this gets out Harry's career is finished, whether Holmes clears his name or not."

"There hasn't been a word in any of the newspapers."

"Well, that's some relief, anyway." She looked through the bars at her husband, who was straining his shoulders against his bonds in an apparent attempt to relax his stiff muscles. Mrs. Houdini continued, "Have you and Sherlock Holmes made any progress? Have you turned up any clues in our favour? You seem to be the only people in London who believe that Harry is innocent."

"Holmes is confident," I assured her. "I shouldn't be surprised if he isn't discrediting the case against your husband even now." I went on to describe our encounter with Mycroft Holmes at the Diogenes Club, which seemed to interest Mrs. Houdini greatly.

"Mycroft Holmes?" she asked. "And he works at Whitehall, you said? Very well. Harry, I'll be back in an hour or so. Franz will be here at two. Dr. Watson, I hope to see you when this business is concluded. I'm off to Whitehall."

"But Mrs. Houdini," I said, "Mycroft Holmes is—" But the resolute woman was already at the far door, calling for the guard to let her out.

"You may as well save your breath, Dr. Watson," Houdini told me, "Bess is determined to clear my name even if she has to speak to the prime minister himself. If your Mycroft Holmes is anywhere in London, she'll find him."

"I don't doubt it, but I suspect she's let herself in for more than she knows with Holmes's brother."

"Maybe not, Watson. I have a brother of my own, you know. His name is Theo. Theo Hardeen, the Wizard of Handcuffs."

"I don't believe I'm familiar with the name," I allowed.

"No one else is either, Doctor, that's Theo's problem. And those people who do see him remember him only as Houdini's brother. I know he dislikes that, but Mama always said—Mama! Thank God she didn't live to see me like this! Can you imagine? It would have killed her. She was so proud of my success, so proud. And now"—Houdini lowered his eyes—"they say I'm a crook. How can I prove I'm not? I never did a dishonest thing in my life. I earned everything I ever got. Try telling that to your Inspector Lestrade, or to your Mycroft Holmes of the British government."

"You'll be free soon, Mr. Houdini. Sherlock Holmes will vindicate you. You can go to the Diogenes Club and tell Mycroft just what you've told me."

"At one of your exclusive British clubs? Hah! I'm a master at getting out of things, Dr. Watson, not getting in. There are some walls even I cannot pass through."

"I don't understand."

"No? Dr. Watson, my father was a rabbi. I am a Jew. My real name is Erich Weiss. How many American Jews do you suppose one finds in your British clubs, dining with the earls and dukes?"

I considered this for a moment, then I recalled something which Mycroft Holmes had said the previous evening. "Mr. Houdini," I hesitated, "Mycroft Holmes said, that is, I believe he said that your father was a . . . a murderer."

Houdini gave a choked cry and twisted violently in his bonds. "A murderer! My father! Had you known, Dr. Watson! He was the gentlest spirit I ever knew, a holy man!" Houdini paused here, breathing heavily. With an effort, he brought his emotions under control. "My father was forced against his will to fight a duel of honour, after which he fled from Budapest to America so that he would not be persecuted. That is why he was so determined to raise his sons as Americans, though he never truly understood American customs, or even the language. That is why I am proud to be an American, in spite of what you British say about us And can you doubt it? Look at what has happened to me here! Accused of a crime I did not commit, the master of escape rots in jail! Hail Britannia!"

Having delivered himself of this diatribe, Houdini hung his head as if exhausted. After a few moments he recovered himself and raised his head to look at me. His eyes had glazed over once more, and he spoke in absolutely lifeless tones. "Perhaps you had best leave me now, Doctor. Soon it will be time for the guards to let me up for my exercise and meal, and then I will be trussed up again. Tell Sherlock Holmes I am still here. The Great Houdini is still in jail."

I could not bring myself to meet his eyes as I rose to take my leave.

FROM SCOTLAND YARD I went directly to the Cleland Hotel, where the Countess Valenka had taken rooms. Seeing Houdini in such a state had given me an even greater desire to bring this unhappy matter to a close as quickly as could be managed. As I alighted from my cab before the Cleland, I resolved that if the countess knew anything at all which would hasten this conclusion, I would not withdraw until I had discovered it.

The Cleland is one of the smaller, more private hotels of the kind which have now grown lamentably scarce. Operated for more than a century by successive generations of the Cleland family, the hotel is known for its hearty Scots hospitality and for its justifiably famous haggis.* I often had occasion to lodge there during my student days, and it is some indication of my boisterous youth that I am remembered there still. Happily, the staff bears me no ill will, and upon inquiry I was politely directed to the countess's suite of rooms on the third floor. I recall wondering, as I was taken up in the lift, why the countess had forsaken the fashionable hotels in the Strand for this more reclusive and modest dwelling. Perhaps she had grown weary of society,

---

*Haggis is a Scottish dish made from the lungs, heart, and other offal of a sheep or calf, mixed with suet, oatmeal, and seasonings, and boiled in the animal's stomach. One supposes that Watson's Scottish heritage enabled him to tolerate it.

I thought, or perhaps she did not wish her movements to be observed.

In the antechamber of the countess's rooms I was met by a diminutive German handmaiden who, though she was clearly well-bred, spoke a rather tortured and unwilling English. Attempting to communicate the nature of my visit as best I could, I quickly discerned, amid a great flurry of answering gestures, that the countess was indisposed.

The reader will understand that from a very early age I was taught that the right of a woman to find herself suddenly indisposed is sacred and inviolate. Under normal circumstances I should have immediately taken my leave, but the thought of Houdini languishing in his cell pressed me to continue, even at the risk of indelicacy. Using a series of grave facial expressions and gesticulations, I somehow managed to impress the great importance of my visit upon the countess's attendant, and she, with a beautifully eloquent shrug, agreed to present my card to her ailing mistress.

The handmaiden had scarcely left the room before the sound of a most animated discussion issued forth from the countess's bedroom. Though I did not intend to eavesdrop, I could not fail to note that one of the voices undoubtedly belonged to a gentleman. I need hardly point out that a gentleman in the bedroom of a proper lady is acutely irregular. A moment later, the bedroom door opened and Herr Osey, the German diplomat, stepped out.

"Ah, my dear Dr. Watson," he said in his careful English, "how good it is to see you again! A most unexpected pleasure!"

"Yes," I replied with some asperity, "most unexpected."

"I see that you are, ah, surprised to find me here, Doctor. You must allow me to explain."

"I require no explanation, Herr Osey," I said. "I wish only to speak to the countess."

"But that is impossible!" he cried, throwing up his hands.

"The countess is very ill! That is why you found me in her boudoir, Doctor. Do you understand? She will not allow anyone else near her until her private physician arrives from München."

Here again I was treading on very thin ice, for Herr Osey was a highly placed German official. But I did not need Sherlock Holmes to tell me that there was a good deal more here than met the eye, so I continued to press my suit.

"I am sorry to learn that the countess is unwell," I said, "but I must see her. I wish only to ask her a few questions on behalf of Mr. Holmes. A man's freedom may depend upon it."

"It is quite impossible," Herr Osey said firmly.

"Then I shall wait here until it becomes possible."

He eyed me carefully. "A gentleman would not insist."

"There are many things which a gentleman would not do," I said pointedly, nodding towards the countess's chamber, "but you forget that I am also a doctor, and may be of some assistance."

"But I've already told you, she refuses to see any British doctor. She will see only her personal doctor."

"That's absurd!" I cried. "If he is coming all the way from Munich it may take a week for him to arrive. I'm certain that I can be of some use to the countess in the interim. If she does not wish to see me, so be it. But I should prefer to hear that from her own lips."

Herr Osey faltered, evidently seeking further arguments to dissuade me, but seeing that I remained firm he had no choice but to consent.

"Very well, Dr. Watson, I will see what I can do." I stood at the window until Herr Osey reappeared to take me in to the countess.

"She really is feeling quite weak," he said. "I don't know what it is that you wish to ask her, but I'm afraid she may not be able to speak at all."

Indeed, I was not certain myself just what it was that I

wished to ask the countess, save that I was to determine the state of her affections for the prince. This would have been a tricky business even under the best of conditions, but now my task was complicated by her apparent ill health and by the unexpected presence of the German diplomat. I have some experience with women, as Holmes is so fond of reminding me, but this situation was quite foreign even to me, and I had no idea of what to expect as Herr Osey ushered me into the countess's presence.

As we passed through a set of French doors, I was immediately struck by the outlandish decor of the chamber in which I found myself. Clearly the countess had imported all her own furnishings, for they in no way reflected the stolid tastes of the Cleland. Neither was the effect at all European, but rather an uncomfortable blending of oriental and Epyptian fancies. Colourful paper lanterns depended from the ceiling, delicate vases, scrolls, and fans filled every shelf and table surface, and at the center of the room stood a fourfold painted silk screen which showed a large silvery spider luring a moth to its doom.

"Have a seat, Dr. Watson," said Herr Osey, closing the doors behind us, "the countess will join us in a moment."

I stepped further into the room and was all but overwhelmed by the thick atmosphere of sweet incense which poured forth from at least three pots.

"Good heavens!" I cried. "This smoke can't be doing her condition any good! Let me open a window at once!"

"Please do not do so, Doctor," came a feminine voice from behind me. "I find the aroma so very soothing."

I turned about and found myself in the presence of one of the four most exotic women I have ever run across. The ivory miniature in Herr Osey's pocket-watch was but a pale suggestion of the reality, for this was a face that would have thoroughly eviscerated a younger man. Her hair, though pulled back in a severe style, was dark and lustrous, like the brown eyes which were large enough to accommodate both fervor and ideation. A high forehead and strong facial lines gave her a mien of proud self-possession, which was only slightly marred by a perceptibly misdirected nose.

"I am the Countess Valenka," she said, stepping across the room, "and you, of course, are Dr. Vatson. Vat a pleasure it is to meet you! Can you forgif me for keeping you vaiting?" Her accent was thick but pleasing, giving stress to odd syllables.

"It is I who must beg to be forgiven," said I, "for intruding upon you in your present condition."

"Oh, nonsense!" she cried, arching her slender neck. "I am vell enough. Nichlaus tends to exaggerate my little ailments beyond all reason."

"Even so," I said, "I am a doctor, and if you are feeling unwell I may be able to provide some assistance."

"That's very kind, Doctor. Please do not take it amiss if I refuse. It is not I lack confidence in your medical skills, but simply I vould not care to discuss my condition vith a stranger."

Herr Osey stepped forward. "There, Dr. Watson, the situation is just as I told you. The countess wishes to be left alone. Will you leave with me now?"

"Vait, Nichlaus, I did not say that." She gave the diplomat a reproving look. "I vould not think of sending the doctor away so abruptly. After all, it is not often I receive so distinguished a visitor. Imagine! The author of the Sherlock Holmes stories!" She looked back at me. "Ve read your stories in Germany, you know. You haf many, many readers in my country. No, I vouldn't think of sending you away, Dr. Vatson. Please do sit down."

I took a seat near the window while the countess arranged herself on a low divan. She wore a close-fitting floral kimono and Japanese bedslippers, which echoed the eastern flavour of the room, and as she propped herself up on a pile of silk cushions, I noticed a heavy chain of agate and jade about her neck.

"And now ve are comfortable, Doctor, you must tell me everything about this beastly friend of yours, Mr. Sherlock Holmes."

I scarcely knew what to make of this remark. "Beastly?" I asked.

"Vell, yes. Of course. He is an ill-bred churl. I don't see how a man such as yourself can possibly abide him."

"I'm sure I don't know what you mean, Countess."

"Ah, but you do, Doctor, you do. My information comes directly from your writings. I am referring to Mr. Holmes's unforgifable behafiour towards vimen in your stories. Vat is it he vonce said? 'Vimen are not to be trusted, not even the best of them.' Now tell me, Doctor, are these the vords of an honourable man? Tell me, am *I* not to be trusted?"

The countess gave me an injured look which softened into a smile as my face reddened.

"If my friend seems unenlightened in his treatment of the fair sex," I ventured, "it is perhaps because he so rarely encounters a woman as enchanting as yourself."

The countess laughed gaily. "Tactfully done, Doctor," she said, again displaying her radiant smile. "I see that you are as clefer in person as you are on the printed page. Vell" —she scooped up a snow-white Siamese kitten which had been playing near the foot of the divan—"let us forget Sherlock Holmes for the moment. Let us talk instead of you. Vy haf you come to see me, Dr. Vatson? Can it be I am suspected in this little mystery up at Gairstowe?"

Again I felt my face grow red. Although I had only just met this woman, she had a way of laying matters open, which I found unsettling. The countess must have read my expression, for she clasped her hands together in obvious glee.

"I *am* !" she cried. "How delightful! Nichlaus, I am a

suspect!" She leaned forward eagerly. "And tell me, Dr. Vatson, am I to be arrested along with this magician fellow?"

"No, Countess," I hastened to assure her, "it is nothing like that. I have merely come to ask some questions on behalf of Mr. Holmes."

"Oh." She looked vaguely chagrined. "Vell, all right then. Vat vould you like to ask me? No!" She held out her hand to forestall any reply I might have made. "No, I vill guess. Yes . . . let me see . . ." She resumed stroking the kitten, which was now amusing itself with a length of twine. "You vant to ask me about those bothersome letters, is that it? Of course it is."

I nodded in uncomfortable affirmation. Though I did not know the precise nature of these letters, I had the impression that this interview would soon strain the limits of decorum. Even so, the countess seemed far less reluctant to discuss the matter than I.

"There is very little to tell, Doctor," she began, fingering a piece of jade at her throat, "it vas a simple question of lepidoptera."

"Pardon me?"

"Lepidoptera. Oh, Dr. Vatson, are you not a collector? Vat a shame. There is nothing like it. The net, the chloroform bottle, the pin and plaster. I haf quite a marvellous collection. Do you efer get to München, Doctor? I'd lof for you to see my butterflies."

"I'm sure that would be very pleasant," I said. "But what do your butterflies have to do with the prince?"

"The prince has recently taken up butterflies himself. Yes, a most timely coincidence. I met him at von of those awful occasions of state and I vas absolutely at a loss for something to say. Then someone mentioned my collection to him and, vell, I'm afraid he rather monopolized me for the rest of the evening. The poor man vas having a misera-

ble time classifying a perfectly basic laceving he'd spotted
somevere in Scotland. He doesn't capture them, you know,
he just obserfs them through field glass. He's only a dab-
bler, really, not very knowledgeable at all. That's vhy he
needed me."

"You exchanged information, then?"

"Yes, ve wrote letters to each other, and ven the prince
next came through Germany he stopped to see my collection. But soon ve began to talk of other things besides the
butterflies, and the prince began coming to Germany more
regularly, and I to England."

The countess smiled and seemed on the point of adding
something, but then merely glanced down at her kitten.

"You were about to say something, Countess?"

"Yes, I vas, but . . . vell . . . I do not care to share all of
the details of my life vith you, Doctor, charming though you
may be. Let us just say the prince . . . the prince made
certain promises . . . certain promises vich he has since
failed to keep. His letters are a clear record of this. I am a
proud woman, Dr. Vatson, and I feel I haf been misused.
And yet it is I who am now shunned by society. There are
vispers and stares as if I vere some sort of . . . of . . ." She
paused in a moment of dismay and her eyes grew moist. She
looked rather like a helpless butterfly herself in her colourful silk robe, fluttering her arms in search of the proper
word. "Vell, never mind all that now. I do not intend to
make trouble. I did, after all, return the letters to him."

"For a price," I reminded her.

"For a just reparation, Doctor." Her eyes now blazed
before she turned away from me. "I am very tired. Please
go now, Dr. Vatson."

"But, Countess—"

"I haf nothing further to say."

Herr Osey took my arm and led me from the room.

* * *

92

I left the Cleland greatly discomfited and in a considerable state of confusion. Though the implication was clear, I refused to believe that His Royal Highness could have committed any such indiscretion.

I walked distractedly along the back streets of Westminster, heading in the general direction of Baker Street, as I tried to puzzle out what had occurred. Why was the countess being kept out of sight, and at whose behest? Why had Herr Osey behaved so strangely, and why had he objected so strongly to my seeing the countess? What was the connection between the two of them, and how did it bear on the intrigue with the prince? These questions so occupied me that it was some time before I noticed a mysterious figure walking along the street nearly one hundred yards behind me. At first I dismissed it as a trick of my imagination, but as I wound through the markets in Oxford Circus, taking a series of arbitrary detours, I could not escape the conclusion that I was indeed being followed. He was a large man, wrapped in a heavy cloak and wearing a broad brimmed hat pulled low over his face. I paused at a book stall and tried to get a better look at him, but he had a long red muffler wrapped about his face, hiding his features from view. Who he was or what he hoped to gain by following me I could only guess, but the fact remained that he was following me and I proposed to do something about it.

Holmes would have easily shaken this pursuer in the back alleys and twisting paths that he knew so well, but I lacked his intimate knowledge of London's byways. Still, I did my best to elude the man in the crowded market-place, but each time I turned another corner or struck out in a new direction, a glance over my shoulder or a brief reflection in a shop window confirmed that he was still behind me.

At length my circuitous path led me out of Oxford Street and into the less populated Cavendish Square. Here we were nearly alone on a long stretch of the avenue, and so it was that I decided to stop running and confront my pursuer. I whirled round and called out a challenge, but the figure reared up and headed down a side-street, evidently unwilling to risk a confrontation with me. I gave chase and very soon we were back on Oxford Street, where the figure now attempted to lose me by darting in and out of the thick crowds.

By now my old war injury had begun to ache, but still I increased my speed, nearly upsetting a fruit cart as I dashed after him. Even so I could barely keep him in sight, and as I attempted to push myself still harder, my leg gave out completely and I tumbled forward onto the pavement.

I was not seriously hurt, but it was clear that my pursuit was at an end, and as a half dozen or so of the passers-by helped me to my feet, I was just able to make out the broad brim of my quarry's hat rounding a distant corner.

HOLMES REAPPEARS

I WAS STILL somewhat shaken when I returned to Baker Street. I am not accustomed to being followed about London by men with disguised features, and I found the experience most disquieting. Settling myself before the fire, I pondered the events of the past two days and attempted to distill some sort of logic from them. First there was the threat against Houdini and his fallacious imprisonment. Then we became aware of the Gairstowe theft and its diplomatic entanglements. And now, finally, there was my curious interview with the Countess Valenka and the subsequent adventure in Oxford Circus. Again and again I turned these events over in my mind, though I could see little where Holmes would no doubt see so much. But as my companion had not yet returned from his mysterious errand of that morning, I was left alone with my speculations and doubts.

By midday I was quite exhausted with this fruitless theorizing, and so I passed the remainder of the afternoon attempting to divert myself with a book of sea stories. As this distraction proved futile I stepped round to my club for a light supper, checking all the while to be certain I was no longer being shadowed. After dining I was invited to play a few rubbers of whist with my clubmates, who took advantage of my obvious preoccupation to bet heavily against me. Returning home in no very sweet humour I found Holmes still absent. I waited past midnight before retiring, and when at last I did fall asleep my dreams were troubled with the image of Houdini lashed to his chair in that most outlandish fashion, imploring aid which I could not give.

I arose the next morning red-eyed and ill-tempered. I snapped unnecessarily at Mrs. Hudson when she laid breakfast for two, and left instructions that I did not wish to be disturbed for the rest of the day. That morning and most of the afternoon were spent pacing about our rooms, smoking no fewer than seven cigars, and imagining at every turn that I heard Holmes's tread upon the stair. My thoughts continued to dwell upon the case, though I had long since given up trying to make sense of it. Rather, my thoughts were those of one who, upon hearing a snatch of melody drift through an open window, cannot resist the attempt to construct an entire concerto in his head.

By late afternoon I had fallen asleep in my chair, and was thus startled several hours later when Holmes burst into the room and shook me roughly by the shoulders.

"What's this, Watson? Asleep? Why have you not visited with Houdini? Why have you not interviewed the countess?" He busily set to relighting the fire which I had allowed to go out.

"I've done all of that," I replied sleepily, "that was yesterday. You have been away for more than a day, Holmes."

"I have?" he asked with an incredulous laugh. "So I have! Marvellous!"

Coming awake, I examined Holmes closely. His eyes were rimmed with red above his unshaven cheeks, and his hair was even more wildly askew than was usual. He was wearing a soiled motoring outfit which I had never seen before, and his hands bore traces of some sort of black inunction.

"Where have you been?" I asked, old fears rising within me. "What have you been doing?"

"Ah, Watson," he sighed, slumping heavily onto the sofa, "I have been in the clouds! Ascending the brightest heaven of invention . . . of cabbages and kings . . ." his voice trailed off.

It was now plain to me that Holmes had been on one of his notorious cocaine binges, and I knew that soon the blackest fit of depression would be upon him. "Holmes! How could you behave so irresponsibly?" My voice quivered with emotion. "With all that is at stake! Houdini is wasting away in the gaol! The prince himself is relying on your discretion—"

"It is on their behalf that I have acted," Holmes said languidly. "You must not shy away from sensation, Watson. It keens the faculties." He waved his fingertips in the air.

How often had I warned him of the destructive effects of this drug? I could not bear to think of that splendid mind being eroded by countless indulgences. Grimly, I made to unbutton his shirt cuff that I might examine his arm for puncture marks.

"What?" he murmured, pulling his arm free. "Oh no, Watson, it is not that. Your vigilance has not been betrayed. No, it is the thrill of the hunt which stimulates me now. Our quarry is of a most inventive stamp, Watson. His trail has pressed me to great heights. Great heights indeed. I find it very rewarding."

Though my suspicions were not entirely lulled, I found my concern returning to the case. "Who is the criminal, then?"

"You musn't expect miracles from me, Watson," he replied, a trifle hurt. "Houdini is the magician, not I. The villain's name is as yet unknown to me. But my net is drawing tight about him, and soon . . ." He curled his bony fingers and held them aloft. "But enough of that. Tell me what you have learned from the countess."

He listened eagerly as I gave a brief account of my visit to the Cleland and of the incident which followed.

"Ah," said Holmes when I had finished, "our friend with the red muffler has attached himself to you, has he? You should be flattered, Watson!"

"What? Do you mean you know him?"

"Well, let us say I've seen him about. He followed us home from the Diogenes the other night, and he caught up with us again after our trip to Gairstowe House. When you and I separated I managed to shake him off by jumping out of a moving four-wheeler."

"But who is he? What does he want?"

"What an inquisitive fellow you are, Watson! It's a pity you weren't quite so persistent with the countess or we might be a good deal closer to our solution."

"What do you mean, Holmes? I learned as much as could be hoped under the circumstances. I thought I did rather well."

"No, Watson, I'm afraid you are too easily intoxicated by feminine allure. It is perhaps your greatest failing. You are more concerned with the cut of a gown than with the poisoning of a husband. True, your narrative holds one or two points of interest, but on the whole you are too chivalrous to be of any real use."

"See here, Holmes, this was a situation which called for the greatest delicacy. Had I been any more direct in my questioning I would have been ejected even sooner. I'm certain you wouldn't have fared any better."

"Perhaps not, but at any rate we'll know soon enough, for I intend to pay a visit to the Cleland at the earliest opportunity. But as it is now rather late to go calling, I suggest we leave the countess until morning. For the present, I have a rather different social outing in mind."

"That suits me perfectly well," I said. "I have been sitting about here for more than a day."

"And I'm afraid you shall have to stagnate here a while longer," Holmes said. "Tonight's expedition is another in which you will not be participating. It is a rather—"

"Holmes, if I am not going along then you shall not go yourself."

"My dear fellow—!"

"I shall not sit by any longer while Houdini remains locked up at Scotland Yard. I cannot bear it." I went on to describe the dreadful circumstances of Houdini's imprisonment.

"Dear me!" Holmes said, "That's bad. Very bad. Well, it shouldn't be much longer."

"Not if I have any part in it," said I. "Now, what is our errand this evening?"

"Watson," Holmes began, his face quite grave, "this business tonight may involve, well, burglary. Though our cause is just, we shall nonetheless place ourselves on the wrong side of the law. Are you still inclined to join me?"

"I stand firm."

"Good fellow!" he cried, clapping my shoulder. "Still, I find your eagerness a bit worrisome. Perhaps I have been looking too far afield for the Gairstowe thief."

Though Holmes attempted to make light of the situation, he was plainly uneasy over involving me in any wrongdoing. Rather than argue the point with him I simply kept quiet and waited, knowing that my willingness would soon outweigh his concerns. In any event, I had no intention of letting him out of my sight until I was certain that he had not resumed his use of narcotics.

At length Holmes appeared to reach a decision, and with a shrug of resignation he leaned forward to confide his plan.

"Do you recall the footprints in Lord O'Neill's study which so engaged our attention?"

"Yes, I do."

"We know that those prints were made by Houdini's shoes. If we accept that Houdini's feet were not in them—"

"Then someone else got hold of a pair of his shoes. Where have we run across that before, eh, Holmes?"*

"Precisely. Now, I have already ascertained that the shoes could not have been taken from Houdini's hotel room. Therefore we must attempt to steal a pair from his dressing-room at the Savoy."

"Why not simply ask Mrs. Houdini for the shoes?"

"Because it will be much more informative to steal them. If we cannot contrive to do so, we will have learned that the shoes were taken by someone with a more ready access to the theatre. This would suggest an employee of the Savoy, or a member of Houdini's own company."

"And if we are successful?"

"Then we will have gone a long way towards shaking the conviction of Lestrade's case against Houdini."

"Very good. I shall fetch the dark lantern."

"We'd best put on our rubber-soled shoes as well. And Watson—"

"Yes?"

"Better slip your service revolver into your pocket." He placed a hand upon my arm. "There may be—"

"I understand. Anything else?"

"Well, yes," he said, touching the bell, "some cold sandwiches before we depart would not go amiss."

*Watson is probably referring to *The Hound of the Baskervilles*, in which a boot was stolen to put the hound on the scent.

· XII ·
WE BECOME CRIMINALS

WITHIN THE HOUR we had arrived in the Strand and were attempting to gain entrance to the theatre. The front doors were heavily secured and the entire building was dark. This cheerless atmosphere was deepened by the few remaining Houdini posters, which were either torn or patched with cancellation notices.

We made our way down the side alley and found the stage door bolted as well. "How shall we get in?" I whispered, though in truth there could not have been anyone there to hear me.

"Let us try to be as resourceful as our thief, Watson," said Holmes, extracting from his pocket a leather case which he opened to display a shining row of metal tools.

"Good heavens, Holmes! Those are burglars' tools! Lock picks!"

"Quite right," he said, bending over the door lock. "Though I may not cause Houdini to look over his shoulder, I do have a certain facility with the common lock. Hold the lantern just there, Watson. This shouldn't take but a moment."

Holmes could not be accused of false modesty in assessing his own locksmithing skills, for the detective spent nearly a quarter of an hour working at that lock, grunting all the while, until at long last we heard a sharp click and the door swung inward.

"The lock was stiff," Holmes said testily, as we stepped into the darkened theatre.

Playing the lantern across the backstage area we could see many large crates and other, more irregular shapes, all covered with oilcloth against the theatre dust. Moving cautiously past the battens and counterweights, we soon came upon the broken remains of the Water Torture Cell, glinting ominously in the lantern light, and beyond that stood the imposing solid brick wall.

"Nothing's been moved since Houdini's arrest," I whispered. "The wall is just where he left it."

"Yes," came the low reply, "but if you've no objection we'll just walk around it rather than through. It's simpler that way."

"But why do you suppose—good heavens! What is that?" I aimed the light at a sudden movement by the rear curtains.

"Rats," answered Holmes. "Come this way." We crossed the dark stage and made our way into a short corridor of rooms off the far wings. "Houdini's dressing-room is the first on the left. See what you can find."

"Where are you going?" I asked, but Holmes placed a cautionary finger to his lips and turned away. Alone, I crept into the room he had indicated and began my examination.

Houdini's dressing-room was small and conspicuously free of the vanities of his profession. A rack in the corner held a blue greatcoat and a modest straw hat. In the closet were four black suit jackets, three with detachable sleeves, and eight pairs of matching trousers which showed considerable wear at the knee. There were two swimming costumes and a dressing-gown, all neatly hung and carefully arranged, and on the floor of the closet sat the objects of our visit—five identical pairs of shoes. I selected the oldest of these and slipped them under my arm.

Turning my attention away from the closet, I noted that Houdini's fastidiousness extended to his dressing-table, where he kept only those personal articles which were strictly necessary, and far fewer of those than I myself was accustomed to using. Where one might have expected to see a vanity case or a make-up kit, Houdini's table held instead a portrait of a venerable old woman, whom I took to be his mother; and crowded about the gold frame were bits of metal coils and springs, a padlock or two, pieces of a broken manacle, and a pair of medieval thumbscrews.

Taking a seat before this peculiar collection, I could not help but ponder the inconsistencies apparent in the character of Harry Houdini. Whereas he had at first seemed unrelievedly brash and pompous, in moments of crisis I had observed concern not for his own safety or comfort, but for the well-being of the craft which he had struggled so tenaciously to perfect. Here in his dressing-room, his personal effects bore no trace of theatrical affectation. Rather, Houdini's private tastes were simple to the point of asceticism, and his only embellishments were those which contributed to his stage persona. Where between the flamboyant performer and the disciplined craftsman did the real Houdini lie?

I was not long in these reflections before the silence of the theatre was broken by a sharp, strident cry which could only have come from Sherlock Holmes.

"Good Lord!" I shouted, rushing from the room. "Are you all right? What has happened?" I weaved my way urgently among the covered crates and backstage curtains, sweeping my lantern frantically across the black space. "Can you hear me? Where are—?"

From out of the darkness a powerful arm encircled my throat and held me fast. The attack came so suddenly that I had no chance to resist, and, as I was pinned from behind, I could not even see my foe.

"Who are you?" snarled a menacing voice, well above my ear. I felt the grip tighten about my throat. "Why are you here?" My lantern clattered to the floor. "Talk! Talk or I'll snap your neck!"

Even in my distress I was able to recognize the clipped

accent of my assailant. "Franz!" my voice came out in a choked gasp. "It is Dr. Watson! Release me!"

"Dr. Watson?" He eased his hold and spun me about as though I were a rag doll. "Oh no! Then that must have been Sherlock Holmes that I pushed down the stairs!"

"What? Holmes!" I bolted forward to the edge of the stage, "Are you all right? Can you hear me? Turn on the light, Franz, I cannot see him!"

Franz dashed to the wings as I called out desperately, straining my eyes against the gloom. "Holmes! Can you hear me? Are you down there?"

"Please do not shout, Watson," came the familiar voice. "My head is not yet recovered from the first onslaught."

"You're all right? You are not injured?"

"I am quite well," he said, "though this has not been my finest hour." At last the lights came up to reveal Holmes seated in the aisle, gingerly touching the back of his head. Franz, greatly relieved that he had not done away with the world's greatest detective, lifted Holmes up and deposited him in the nearest theatre seat.

"Please forgive me, Mr. Holmes," he said anxiously, "I could not see that it was you. You should have telephoned before coming down."

"Yes, well, think nothing of it," Holmes said, wincing as I probed a swelling on the back of his head. "It is no more than I deserved. I trust your reasons for being here are more creditable than our own?"

"Do I need a reason to be here, Mr. Holmes? Where else would I be? In a stuffy hotel room? No, thank you."

"But surely you don't sleep here?" I asked, having satisfied myself that Holmes had suffered no great injury. "Even Houdini does not go so far."

"Only because his wife would not permit it, Doctor," Franz answered. "So the job falls to me. I would not have it any other way. It is the very least that I can do for the Houdinis."

"The very least?" asked Holmes. "It seems to me that Houdini expects rather a lot from you."

"Not at all," Franz returned. "You see, I am far more than just an assistant to Mr. Houdini. Far more. I am his confidant, his . . . his"—Franz thought for a moment—"his Dr. Watson, if you will. Both he and Mrs. Houdini have treated me as family since fate brought us together in Stuttgart."

"Fate brought you together?" Holmes asked. "Fate is not usually so accommodating."

Franz smiled. "Yes, it may seem odd to you, Mr. Holmes, but I am a great believer in fate. I have had . . . I have had an odd life, and if the Houdinis had not found me when they did I would be dead or worse by now."

"Dead or worse?"

Franz nodded. "I make no secret of my past," he began, "but it is not a pleasant story.

"I was born in Stuttgart to an old, established family, and I was bred to a life of idle comfort. But my father died when I was still young, and he left a number of debts behind. My mother tried her best, but she could not save us from ruin. All of our property was taken from us and we were reduced to poverty and disgrace. Within three years my mother, too, was gone." Franz folded his large hands and then unfolded them again. "I was then twenty years old. I had no money, no skills, and only that education which befits a young toff. I was ill-prepared for what lay ahead. The next six years . . . well, suffice it to say that at the end of six years I had sunk very low in the world. I lived from hand to mouth, and worse, I had developed a powerful and consuming addiction to cocaine. The drug made me a madman! I would do anything to satisfy my cravings. Can you understand this? The depravity? Can you imagine the absolute degradation of one's soul?"

Holmes chose not to answer.

"It is a time of my life that, mercifully, I do not remember very well. There are bits and fragments which return to me: Foraging through garbage, sleeping with vermin, striking down an elderly man for his cloak—no, I was not above stealing from others to support myself and my addiction. I would prey upon travellers who had been unwise enough to stray into the waterfront district, the area known as 'Satan's Lair.'

"One night I set upon a young American couple and demanded their money. I did not know it at the time, but they were Mr. and Mrs. Houdini. I had been foolish enough to think that such a small man would be easily overcome. But Mr. Houdini was not intimidated either by my size or by the knife with which I threatened him. Within a second he had knocked me down and seized my knife. I was rendered entirely helpless. And he did not stop there. He took my knife, broke off the blade, and said, 'It's one thing to threaten me, my big friend, but when you threaten my wife, that is a different matter.' To make a long story short, the Houdinis saw me cured of my addiction and restored to health, and when the time came for them to return to America, I went with them."

Franz reached into his pocket and withdrew the broken handle of a parang knife. "This is all that remains of the life I once led. And that, gentlemen, is how I met the man that Scotland Yard now calls a thief. Houdini is not a thief! He is a reformer of thieves!"

"That is a very remarkable story, Franz," I said.

"Yes, it is," Holmes agreed. "And you have travelled with Houdini ever since?"

"Yes, for four years. They have been the best four years I have ever known. Soon these ridiculous accusations against Mr. Houdini will be proven false, and he will perform again. He will find that I have everything ready." Franz looked about the theatre proudly. "All will be ready."

Holmes stood up and rubbed at the back of his head. "Perhaps you can help us to hasten that day, Franz. Your capacity here may be of use to us."

"Of course! I will do anything I can! I would walk to the end of the earth to straighten this matter out!"

"That won't be necessary. All I require is information."

"Ask me anything you like."

"You have been in the theatre every night since Houdini's arrest?"

"Every night since we arrived in England. Someone must stay with the show at all times. These secrets are the most sought after in all of vaudeville. We must maintain our guard."

"Excellent," said Holmes, "and in that time have there been any intruders? Perhaps more accomplished ones than Dr. Watson and myself?"

Franz laughed heartily. "Yes, Mr. Holmes. You British are no different from the Americans when it comes to Houdini's secrets. I have not caught anyone, but I have seen the signs."

Holmes's eyes grew bright. "What signs?"

"Oh, things not in their places. The coverings disturbed."

"Any disorder in Houdini's dressing-room?"

Franz regarded my companion with a puzzled look. "Yes, in fact, though what anyone hoped to discover in there is beyond me."

"Would you show us what was disturbed?" Holmes asked eagerly.

"Certainly, if you think it's important," Franz said, leading us back onto the stage. "Just a moment, I'll find the light for the backstage area."

While he went to turn on the light, I stepped over to where my dark lantern had fallen, and it was there that I made a most distressing discovery. Still a bit shaky from

Franz's choking hold, I steadied myself on one of the covered packing crates as I bent to retrieve the lantern. When I stood up I found my hand unaccountably sticky. It was then that I noticed an odour which, as a physician, I knew only too well.

"Holmes," I said quietly.

"In a moment, Watson. We must see—"

"Holmes."

"Very well, Watson, what—" As he stepped closer, he too perceived the odour. Without another word he uncovered the crate, but found that it was padlocked.

"Franz!" cried the detective. "We must open this trunk!"

"I cannot, Mr. Holmes. That is Mr. Houdini's famous metamorphosis substitution trunk, one of his most jealously guarded secrets."

Again Holmes withdrew his burglars' tools and set to work on the lock with a grim determination.

"All right, Mr. Holmes," said Franz. "Don't do that. You'll only damage it." He produced a set of keys and unfastened the lock.

"*Oh Istenem!*" he cried, raising the lid. "This is terrible! Terrible!"

There in the trunk was heaped the body of a young woman, hideously strangled with a length of steel chain. The chain had been drawn so tightly about her neck that it bit deeply into the empurpled flesh, and sent crimson streaks upward towards a face of such remarkable beauty that even the ravages of violent death could not entirely disfigure it.

"Holmes," I whispered hoarsely, "who is this unfortunate creature?"

Holmes turned to me in ashen-faced surprise. "What? You do not recognize her?" He looked again at the figure in the trunk. "Watson, this is the Countess Valenka!"

· XIII ·
MURDER AND BREAKFAST

"Now let's see if I can get this clear," said Lestrade at breakfast the next morning. "The woman in the trunk is the Countess Valenka, that much is certain. But if the countess has been dead all this time, who was Watson speaking to at the Cleland the other day?"

"What can you mean, Lestrade?" I asked. "I'm quite certain that I was addressing the countess herself."

"And yet you failed to recognize her when you discovered her body at the theatre?"

"Is it any wonder that I did not immediately recognize her in the trunk? After all, there was considerable damage. She had been strangled to death!"

"True, but it's a very important point," Lestrade said, reaching across for the eggs. "You see, I don't believe you ever spoke to the countess at all."

"I assure you I did!"

"You only *think* you did, Dr. Watson. I don't know who it was that you spoke to at the Cleland, but at that point the countess was already dead, killed by Houdini."

"You can't mean that, Lestrade!" I cried.

"But I do! It's perfectly clear that the murder conforms exactly to my early conjectures—confirms them, I should say. The body was found right in our suspect's trunk! I should be very dull indeed if I failed to see a connection. Don't you agree, Holmes?"

The detective set down his teacup. "Let us say I am reserving my judgement."

"Oh, come now, Mr. Holmes," Lestrade retorted. "Dr. Watson himself was unable to fix the time of death precisely, save to confirm that the body had been in that trunk for more than twelve hours. It's obvious that she was dead before we took Houdini into custody."

"But I tell you I spoke to the countess the following day!"

"How can you be so certain that you saw her alive, Doctor, when you failed to recognize her dead?"

"But then who did I speak with at the Cleland? If it was not the countess, why did Herr Osey tell me it was?"

"I will ask him when I find him, Doctor. He has been summoned back to Germany on government matters."

"You don't find that at all curious? Are you so determined to convict Houdini that you are blind to all other suspects? Why has Herr Osey left the country so precipitously? For that matter, why haven't you questioned Houdini's assistant, Franz? He had access to the trunk!"

"Don't worry, Dr. Watson. I always make certain of my facts. Herr Osey's summons was official. I confirmed it myself. As for the assistant, he makes a poor suspect. He had neither the motive nor the opportunity. I looked into that story he told you, it's all true. He is what he says he is. What's more, he fainted dead away at the sight of the body! Don't you see, Doctor, the assistant's presence at the theatre is the final proof of my theory. This man Franz would have detected any intruders to the theatre, just as he did you and Holmes. Therefore, no one could have placed the body in Houdini's trunk without his knowledge. No one, that is, but Houdini himself. So you see how neatly it all comes together." Lestrade sat back and dabbed at his lips with a napkin.

I looked at Holmes in despair, but the detective remained silent.

"Look, I'll explain from the beginning," Lestrade continued. "We already have Houdini for the theft of the Gairstowe papers. Now this countess—another German, mind you, and a theatre person to boot—turns up dead in his trunk. I suppose I shouldn't tell you this," he leaned forward confidentially, "but it is my understanding that the murdered woman was very much involved with the documents which are now missing."

"You don't say?"

"It is so. No doubt that is why Houdini had to kill her."

"But to place the body in his own trunk! Surely only the clumsiest of murderers would dispose of a body in this fashion?"

He probably knew we'd never look in that trick trunk of his. Or, more likely, he planned to move the body later but was taken before he could do so." He stroked his whiskers thoughtfully. "Yes, that's probably it."

"But why murder the countess at all?"

"I suspect she was in on the theft. Perhaps she was threatening to expose Houdini. We are looking into the possibility that they were . . . acquainted."

"Surely not!" I cried. "Houdini's wife assures us that he is a most devoted husband."

"Well, she would say that, wouldn't she?" Lestrade gave a knowing wink. "Look, Doctor, I'll spell it out plain as day. Even if there were no footprints, we should have soon reasoned that Houdini was the only person at Gairstowe House capable of penetrating the vault. Now we find this Countess Valenka's body in his trunk. And how was she murdered? By a chain wrapped tightly around her neck, and locked in place with one of Houdini's own padlocks. Suppose, Dr. Watson"—Lestrade threw down his napkin and began to pace the room—"suppose that you were to murder someone in this manner. Say you and I have robbed a bank, and have just now returned to Baker Street to divide the proceeds. At some time in the course of our negotiations, you become angry with me and decide to kill me without delay. You cast about for a weapon. In your case, a scalpel or even a poison might come to hand. But suppose you were Houdini, and our argument were taking place down at the Savoy? You see a length of chain from one of your escapes lying close by. You snatch it up and wrap it about my throat, but then what happens?"

"I can't imagine."

"Think, man! Here you are, strangling me with a chain," Lestrade bulged his eyes and made alarming noises in his throat. "It is horrible to see! You've never killed a man before. You suddenly realize, 'Oh no! I am killing my old friend Lestrade!' Still, though you cannot bear to look at my face, you decide to go through with the murder. You pull the chain tight and lock it fast." He pantomimed this motion. "This allows the constriction of the chain to finish me off. But observe, Watson, in the course of locating and fastening the lock, you must surely have taken one of your hands away from my throat. This means that you maintained a choking grip on the chain with only one hand, even against my struggles. May we not assume, then, a murderer of great strength? Might we also assume highly developed coordination, and, I think it safe to say, a functional knowledge of locks? Our friend Houdini possesses all three traits, does he not?" Lestrade picked up his teacup and smiled expectantly at Holmes and myself. "It all makes perfect sense, do you see?"

"What about the mud?" asked Holmes.

"The mud? *The mud?*"

"The mud which made the footprints in Lord O'Neill's study. Where does the mud fit in?"

"Holmes, you haven't heard a word I've said!"

"On the contrary, I have followed you closely. I simply wish to know what provisions you have made for this highly disconcerting mud."

"I fail to see the importance of this mud, Holmes. I have presented what I believe is the correct solution of the case, and you are off on a wild tangent. Very well then, the mud was left by Houdini's shoes, if I must state the obvious."

"How did Houdini's shoes come to be muddy?" Holmes asked, warming to the subject.

"I expect he stepped in a puddle," Lestrade said brusquely.

"Inside of the house?" Now it was Holmes who began to pace. "In order to get from the main ballroom, where Houdini performed his conjuring tricks, to Lord O'Neill's study, one passes through two hallways and up one flight of steps. I have examined these areas, and saw not one mud puddle."

"He must have stepped outside."

"Why?"

"To allay suspicion. To be seen leaving the gathering."

"All right, Lestrade, suppose we accept this premise as fact. We are still faced with three insurmountable difficulties. The first involves the trail of muddy prints in the study."

"Holmes! Where is your mind? It was not a trail, it was more of a grouping."

"Ah! But it should have been a trail. Instead we found nothing leading into or out of the study; only a distinct, isolated grouping of prints behind the desk. You see the problem."

Lestrade did not reply.

"Second, as I have tried repeatedly to impress upon you, I am certain that the mud came from nowhere within the confines of the Gairstowe estate. In fact, I cannot place the mud at all. So, we must assume that Houdini left the gathering, travelled to some distant point where he muddied his shoes, and then returned—perhaps walking on his hands so as to avoid leaving a trail. Why should he do this? How did he get past the guard?"

"Really Holmes, to make so much of a trifle! Can you be so certain of the mud?"

Holmes ignored the question.

"And the third irregularity, Holmes?" I asked. "You mentioned three."

"The ground was dry that night. It had not rained for three days."

"So there would not have been any mud puddles," I reasoned.

"Precisely so."

"Oh, come now!" cried Lestrade, growing quite irritated. "He may well have stepped into a flower-bed, Holmes. A flower-bed filled with moist earth which was not native to the estate. Have you considered that possibility? I don't know what your game is, but I haven't the time for it now. It's all very well for you and Dr. Watson to lose yourselves in these details, but I must have results; and in this instance I must have them before the diplomatic complications become unmanageable." He took down his hat and ulster. "Thank Mrs. Hudson for a lovely breakfast, gentlemen, but I must return to my duties." He paused at the door and raised a finger in admonishment. "I welcome your insights, Holmes, but you must learn to address them to the facts, not your idle theories. They'll lead you nowhere! Good day." He turned and bustled down the steps, slamming the lower door behind him.

"That was an agreeably dramatic exit," commented Holmes. "He is developing quite a flair."

"A flair!" I scoffed. "He is intolerable! He grows more so by the year. Why do you abide him?"

"Actually, Watson, he and Gregson are the best of the lot, and of the two Lestrade has the virtue of honesty." With this equable comment, Holmes began packing his after-breakfast pipe.

I hope the reader will indulge me in my dotage if I digress here for a moment, for I find that the mention of Holmes's pipe affords an opportunity I have long awaited.

In the last twenty years I have seen countless drawings

and other renderings in which a likeness of Sherlock Holmes is shown smoking a large, curved calabash pipe. He is generally seen puffing reflectively on this pipe while explaining some simple point to his elderly, easily befuddled companion. As Holmes and I are the same age, I pride myself that my mind is still keen enough to recollect that he never, to the best of my knowledge, owned a calabash pipe. It was, then, his disreputable old black clay that he smoked upon Lestrade's departure that morning, filling it with all the dottles and plugs left over from his previous day's smokes, lighting it with an ember from the fire, and tamping it down with Mrs. Hudson's silver butter-knife. I myself took a cigar, and waited patiently for Holmes to comment on the murder of the countess.

"Lestrade is correct on one point," Holmes said, replacing the fire-tongs, "and that is that this business must be concluded quickly. No doubt he is under enormous pressure from his superiors to convict Houdini."

"But why?"

"To have the case solved, and more importantly, to have it solved quietly and without scandal. Should it transpire that the countess was murdered by an Englishman, the relations between our countries would become even more strained."

"That would be unfortunate, of course," I said, "but the Yard is on the point of convicting an innocent man! Are the diplomatic worries so very great?"

Holmes did not appear to have heard. He walked to the window and stood motionless for a long while, staring down at Baker Street. But for the staccato puffs of smoke rising from his pipe, I should have mistaken him for the wax bust which briefly occupied that space some years earlier.*

---

*Very briefly. It was almost immediately smashed by a bullet from Colonel Sebastian Moran's airgun.

"Watson," he said at last, turning away from the window. "Are you still as eager for the chase? Would you undertake a brief journey on my behalf?"

"Of course," I answered. "I had planned to visit Houdini again, but seeing this morning's headlines, I'm not sure I'd have the heart to face him."

Holmes took the newspaper I held out to him. " 'American Magician Accused of Murder,' " he read, " 'Theft Suspect Already in Custody.' No, I don't think he'll like that."

"Holmes, it will devastate him. You must solve this case immediately!"

"Very well then, Watson, I shall do as you instruct, but you must participate in the solution."

"Gladly. What am I to do?"

"Fetch your coat, I shall explain in the cab."

Within moments Holmes had secured a hansom and issued instructions to the driver. "Now then," he began, as we lurched off towards Portman Square, "for the time being it will be necessary for me to devote my energies to this latest problem."

"The murder?"

"The murder, yes, but the actual murder itself is not my central concern. What is even more compelling is this uncertainty which surrounds the countess's identity and movements. Her final days must be reconstructed before we can proceed."

"I see. And what is my part in all of this?"

"You shall approach the problem from the opposite direction. Remember, we initially came to this investigation by means of a threat against Houdini. Though the problem has now grown beyond that, we should not lose sight of our original concern."

" 'Tonight who the fraud is we shall see'?"

"Exactly. I have made some inquiries concerning this rival escape artist of Houdini's, Herr Kleppini. I have sa-

116

tisfied myself that he is involved in the Gairstowe crime at least, if not the murder. At present, Kleppini is plying his trade from a booth on the Brighton Pier. I have determined that he performed there on the evening of the crime. I am also told that he conducted a seance the following afternoon. You must—"

Our hansom pulled up sharply. "Victoria!" shouted the driver from on top of the box.

"Come along, Watson," said Holmes, leaping down, "your train leaves in a moment."

"My train?" I asked, hurrying after him.

"Yes. You are going to Brighton," he informed me, leading us through the arch. "If the theft of the letters occurred as I suspect, Kleppini could not have returned to Brighton in time to conduct his afternoon seance." He pulled me along the platform, signalling to the conductor. "You must determine if it is Kleppini himself conducting his afternoon seance, and if so, whether or not it would have been possible for another performer to take his place. Do you understand? Good, off you go!"

"But, Holmes," I said, considerably unsettled by the haste of these arrangements, "is this not a fool's errand? If Kleppini did steal the letters, won't he have disposed of them by now? Why has the scandal you fear not come to pass?"

"Because," said Holmes, hastening me into a coach as two short whistles sounded, "I have discovered that there is one letter yet remaining in Lord O'Neill's possession. A letter in the countess's own hand, in which she denounces all the others. So long as we have this letter, all the rest are rendered harmless."

"Then why—?" But it was too late, for the train had begun to pull free of the platform, and Holmes was already striding off in the other direction.

· XIV ·
A SEANCE ON THE PALACE PIER

THE JOURNEY by train to Brighton is a pleasant one, made more so by anticipation of the hospitable seaside resort at its end. When Mary was alive, she would frequently bring me down to take the sun and to visit the Brighton Lanes. There, in that twisting, narrow course of antique shops, we would spend many happy hours among the dusty bric-à-brac of the previous century. It was these memories which engaged my thoughts as I alighted in the Brighton station, taking my mind from the less congenial purpose of my present visit.

Leaving the station through the south gates, I strolled briskly down the Queen's Road, pausing only momentarily to glare at the monstrous Royal Pavilion,* and soon I had arrived at the well-known Brighton seashore.

The better travelled of my readers may scoff at the very notion of England boasting a seaside resort, given our rather temperate climate; but on this day the sun was bright, if not actually hot, and I was pleased to find several hundreds of my countrymen disporting themselves there upon the beach. While it is true that Brighton's beach is composed of hard pebble and rock, rather than sand, if one lies out on a wooden deck-chair, wrapped in a wool blanket

---

*George IV's summer palace, an elaborate imitation of the Taj Mahal. Watson probably considered it an inexcusable tax burden; others merely found it hideous.

against the sea chill, it is possible to get a good bit of colour in one's cheeks. Or so my wife always contended, and I never chose to dispute her.

The heavily trafficked section of the Brighton shore is flanked by two marvellous wooden piers, which extend some hundreds of feet into the Channel and are supported by stout wooden piles. The first of these is the West Pier, whose trim, elegant ballroom has housed some of society's grandest summer affairs. The newer of the two, the Palace Pier, has attracted a less desirable patronage. Built at the turn of the century, it has become a haven for gypsies and charlatans, who, in hastily constructed booths ranging up and down the length of the pier, display dubious feats of skill or aberrations of nature, offered less for amusement than for the purpose of separating the labourer from his wages. It was here, amid this mean and squalid bluster, that I was to seek the mysterious Kleppini.

Paying my three shillings at the rotting turnstile, I pushed my way into the crowd and out onto the pier. Among the diversions available that afternoon, each heralded by a garishly painted signboard, were a "pulse-quickening" display of snake charming, a "mystic fakir" asleep on a bed of nails, and a burly fire-swallower whose demonstration carried the warning: Not for the faint of heart. Picking my way through the eager couples and boisterous youths, I had travelled nearly to the far end of the pier before locating Kleppini's booth.

I had never before seen the man, but I could hardly mistake his signboard, for it proclaimed in bright red letters: Kleppini! The Man Who Humbled Houdini! Houdini's name, I noted, was printed in larger letters than Kleppini's own, and indeed the illustration showed a man who looked rather like Houdini, muscular and compact, bound in heavy irons but preserving a characteristically defiant tilt of the head. Leaning against the feet of this illustration was a hand-lettered notice which announced a seance in ten minutes.

Pushing aside a musty grey curtain, I stepped into a booth which was lit by a single candle. As my eyes adjusted to the gloom, I made out the forms of three other persons seated about a low table in the center of the room, apparently come to avail themselves of Herr Kleppini's spiritualistic gifts. Finding no seats, I lowered myself onto a tattered cushion as the others had done and awaited the entrance of Kleppini. Below us the waves slapped against the supports of the pier, and the smell of rotting fish and algae wafted up through the cracks.

I need hardly say that but for my errand, undertaken on behalf of Sherlock Holmes, I should never have found myself in such a peculiar setting. But once there I awaited the proceedings with great interest, and took advantage of my timely arrival to examine the three others who had come to communicate with the dead.

To my right was a sallow-faced young man in a striped jacket and straw hat. At his side was a samples-case, and I was able to gather by his conversation that he was a commercial traveller making sales calls in Brighton. "These spiritualists," he was explaining to his companion, "are fraudulent without exception, but they provide a certain"—he paused and laid a finger alongside his temple—"intellectual amusement for the truly incisive mind."

His companion, a pale-complexioned schoolgirl of no more than seventeen years, giggled and clutched at his arm in nervous affirmation. "I don't know about any of that," she said, pulling a strand of hair out of her eyes. "I just know that it gives me a bad fright just to think about talking with dead people!"

"That's all right," laughed her young man, pulling her close to him. "That's what I'm here for."

Throughout this exchange the third member of our party

sat by regarding the pair with obvious distaste. This man's dress and manner proclaimed him an active sailor, but his age and physical limitations suggested otherwise, for the bristles which covered his chin were stark white, and though he continually stroked and worried at them with one hand, the other—a hook—remained motionless at his side. As always when in later years I would encounter highly unusual characters in suggestive settings, I examined the sailor for any sign which struck me as familiar, but a scrutiny of several moments left me uncertain as to whether this old salt could possibly be Sherlock Holmes in another of his disguises. Could even Holmes have managed the hook?

My seat, if the crouching position I had assumed on the pillow could be called such, was set very near to a ragged grey screen in the corner of the room. Before long I heard whisperings and jostlings from behind the screen, followed by the sudden appearance of a plump, matronly German woman. This woman stood for some moments appraising our group with tight-lipped disapproval before stepping back behind the screen. The whispering renewed, with the words *"Vier? Nur vier?"* being plainly audible. Then, as if propelled by a shove, the woman reappeared and solemnly addressed the assembled patrons.

"He who is Kleppini is soon appeared," she managed to say in a guttural drone, "for showing the miracles which no man is understanded. But before he is here, you must each to put five shillings here." She held up a brass cup in front of each of us in turn, displaying no emotion as we deposited our coins.

"This is now good," she said, assuming a position before the screen, "for miraculous Kleppini is appeared." With as much drama as she was able to muster, this leaden-faced woman began to shake an African gourd in a steady, insistent tattoo. Evidently this was meant to heighten the suspense of the situation, but when it went on for two full minutes without result, the four of us began to grow restless. Then, at last, Kleppini strode forth with a sweeping flourish and a grateful wave of his hand, by which he seemed to imply that his arrival had been nothing short of miraculous, when in fact he had simply stepped from behind the screen.

"I greet you, I greet you all," he said with a low bow. "I sit down. I sit down with you."

Herr Kleppini was a much smaller and slighter man than the illustration on his signboard had suggested. In fact, he was some inches shorter than Houdini and only half as broad. He wore a pale-blue robe painted with flecking silver stars, and about his head was wound a frayed turban which bore the unmistakable imprint of hotel linen.

'And now," he said, placing his palms on the table, "let us join hands, and together we shall attempt to communicate with the great beyond. Together we shall attempt to cross that stormy chasm which separates our world from theirs, the living from the dead." Kleppini closed his eyes and began to rock his head forward and back, humming loudly. "Great spirits," he chanted, "beings of the night, hear me! Hear Kleppini, who beckons you from the land of the living!"

The humming resumed at an increased volume and Kleppini's head continued to rock back and forth. "Great spirits . . . great spirits . . . wait!" Kleppini sat upright and stared off across the room. "I sense another presence! I sense that the spirits are here with us now! O Spirits, let me be the vessel through which you speak! Let me be thy voice!" With a final burst of frantic humming, Kleppini's head slumped forward onto the table.

For a moment the four of us sat in silence, hands still joined, staring apprehensively at the slumped figure at the head of the table.

"Perhaps he's gone and died himself," suggested the young salesman.

"Quiet!" his lady friend remonstrated. "He's trying to reach the spirits!" She leaned towards Kleppini solicitously. "Mr. Kleppini? Are you all right? Can we help you in some way?"

Suddenly reanimated, Kleppini threw his head back and gave a deep, raucous laugh. "I am not Kleppini!" he roared in a gruff voice. "I am not the good and gentle Kleppini! I am Lord Maglin! The *late* Lord Maglin! I have returned from the dead to be with you here today. See how the very room trembles at my presence!"

The grey curtain and the table began to quiver, as if in fear.

"It's a fake," whispered the young salesman. "He's rattling the table himself! His wife's doing the curtain!"

"Silence!" Kleppini shouted. "Lord Maglin commands silence! It is not your place to question the workings of the spirit world! These are riddles which no living man may comprehend!"

From behind the screen a trumpet bleated. A moment later the instrument itself appeared to dance above our heads.

"It's on a wire!" the salesman insisted. "The trumpet's on a wire!"

"I command silence!" Kleppini repeated, still in the voice of Lord Maglin. "The spirits will not abide disbelievers!"

"Do be quiet, Willard," the young lady urged of her companion. "I want to see what happens!"

"You'd best listen to your young friend," Kleppini advised darkly. "She knows the power of the spirit world. She knows the great . . . mystery." A ghostly hand appeared suspended over our heads and then vanished. The young lady screamed at the sight of it. "Now," Kleppini resumed, "who will ask a question of Lord Maglin, the prince of the spirit world? Do not be afraid! The past, the present, and the future are all one to me here. The loved ones you have lost, they are all here with me now, and the riddles of the ages are made plain. Ask what you will. You, sir"—he indicated the sailor with a broad gesture—"what is your question for the spirits?"

The sailor, who had declined to join hands with the rest of us, slowly placed his hook upon the table. "Well, I'm not sure I—"

"Put aside your fears," Kleppini urged. "Just as the spotted lizard writhes upon the hot sands of destiny, truth is within your grasp. Ask what you will."

"Well"—the sailor coughed and stroked his bristled chin —"there was this mate I had once, he fell overboard just off Spitsbergen—"

"Yes, yes," Kleppini intoned, "and you wish to speak to him. Very well. The black wolf which howls at the moon of providence smiles upon us. Your friend approaches now." A ghostly tapping sound filled the room, followed by the rattling of chains. "Listen . . . he comes. He comes. Call out to him."

"McMurdo?" called the sailor tentatively. "Are you there?"

"Yes, it is I, McMurdo," said Kleppini, his voice now ghostly and tremulous. "It is good to hear your voice again, my friend. There is much to tell you. I see what the future holds for you. I see a great many things. You will . . . you will give help to a stranger . . . and he . . . he will reward you. He will reward you beyond your fondest dreams. Yes, that is what will happen. . . . And wait! I see more . . . you . . . you will be . . . very happy." Kleppini's head sank forward in exhaustion.

"That's it?" cried the sailor, brandishing his hook in the air. "Help to a stranger? Rewarded? There has to be more than that!"

"I am sorry," Kleppini answered, once again in the voice of Lord Maglin. "Darkness veils the third eye of the spider."

"But—But—"

Kleppini silenced him with a gesture. "Who else will ask a question of the spirits?"

The pale young girl spoke up. "I would like to ask a question, O Spirits," she said with great reverence. "Will they speak to me?"

With a solemn nod, Kleppini resumed his tuneless humming at an increased volume. "Yes, yes, as the golden fish swims through the crystal waters of tomorrow, the fates reveal themselves to me. Who is it you would speak with across the spirit divide?"

"I—I have an aunt," the girl stammered, turning a shade paler, "Aunt Gwyneth. I'd like to speak with her, if it please you."

"Gwyneth?" Kleppini intoned. "Yes, Gwyneth is here with us now. Even now she struggles to be heard." Kleppini inclined his head and the chamber was again filled with ghostly tapping.

"Hello?" Kleppini's voice came in a wispy falsetto. "Hello? Is that my niece? Am I speaking to my own dear girl?"

"Yes, Aunt Gwyneth!" cried the girl, considerably awed. "It's me, Isabel!"

"Isabel, my darling! It is so good to be with you again. I have something to tell you. Something very important . . . but wait! Wait! The mists grow heavier! I cannot hear you. . . . Are you still there, Isabel?"

"Yes, yes, I'm here," Isabel said.

"I'm afraid for you, my dear. I'm afraid that this young man you've taken up with is the wrong sort. His kind bring nothing but trouble. He is a . . . a disbeliever!"

"A disbeliever?"

"Yes! He'll bring you grief, my dear. Nothing but grief!"

"Then what am I to do?" asked the gullible young lady.

"A stranger will show you a kindness," answered the falsetto, "and you will see the way."

"Don't listen to this nonsense," said the young man, pulling at her arm. "Come on, let's get away from here."

"No, leave me alone." She pulled her arm away. "Aunt Gwyneth? A stranger, you said?" But Kleppini's head had slumped forward once more. "Now see what you've done, Willard!"

"I've had enough of this," Willard answered. "We're leaving."

"I'm not leaving with you," sniffed the girl. "Not with a disbeliever like you. I'll see myself home. Or better still, I'll ask this kind gentleman to see me home." To my great dismay, she looped her arm through my own and rested her pallid cheek on my shoulder. "Yes! 'A stranger will show you a kindness!' It's happened already!"

"Now see here, young lady—" I began.

"Him?" The young man was outraged. "You must be joking! He's sixty if he's a day! Come back over here where you belong!"

"Don't you pay any attention to him, sir," the girl told me. "He's a jealous one. What's your name, then?"

"John Watson, but you—"

"John Watson?" asked the old sailor, who had been silent all this time. "Say, you're not Dr. Watson, are you? The friend of Sherlock Holmes? The one who writes the stories?"

"Well, I am, but—"

"Dr. Watson?" Kleppini was instantly alert. "You are Dr. Watson? We are honoured to have you with us, sir. What would you ask of the spirits? A question from Sherlock Holmes, perhaps?"

"No, I just . . . I have no question."

"Wait! Lord Maglin will tell us your trouble! Lord Maglin knows all! He will see to the heart of this problem." The trumpet sounded again from behind the screen. "I am concentrating, concentrating, but it is so hard! So very hard!" He groaned tragically. "I must cast the beacon of my mind through layer after layer of the darkness of tomorrow."

With a sigh, I placed a handful of coins into the brass cup. In recognizing me, the sailor had unwittingly compromised my errand for Holmes, but for the present there was nothing for it but to hear Kleppini out.

"Ah . . . good . . ." Kleppini said, "good." He hummed for a moment and then, as if struck by a thunderbolt, he opened his eyes and stared across the table at me. "There has been a murder done! A terrible, terrible murder!"

The young salesman scoffed. "I read about that in the newspapers this morning! I knew about it already!"

"Be patient, I begin to see more . . . hark! Houdini is involved! The upstart Houdini, impudent rival of the great Kleppini! He is the villain, and what is this? The great detective Sherlock Holmes is acting on his behalf!"

I made to speak but Kleppini silenced me with a gesture. "Oh, I see it all now," he gasped. "I see everything. Houdini, he has stolen some secret documents from the government of this fine country and . . . oh! Dare I say it? The woman he murdered, she was a noblewoman! A countess! And Houdini killed her!"

"Is this true, Dr. Watson?" asked the girl fearfully.

"Certainly not," I began. "Certainly not—!"

"Hark!" cried Kleppini. "Hark! All will be plain soon enough, for here is the countess herself! She comes to speak with us! The murdered woman comes!" Kleppini fell silent as the rattling chains and tapping noises swelled through the room again. Now, even I began to feel a trifle anxious, though I had been long since convinced of the fraudulent nature of the seance.

"Dr. Watson?" came Kleppini's falsetto. "Dr. Watson, it is I, the Countess Valenka!"

The voice, like the one belonging to Aunt Gwyneth, was tremulous and ghostly.

"Dr. Watson . . . take pity on a murdered woman! Please, I beg you . . . see that justice is done!" The voice quivered tragically. "Sherlock Holmes has made a mistake! He thinks that Houdini is innocent, but he is wrong! Houdini stole the papers! He stole them! And then . . . oh! And then he murdered me! Oh, take pity, Dr. Watson! You are a good man, take pity!"

This slanderous dupery was more than I could bear. "Stop it, Kleppini!" I cried, leaping to my feet. "Stop this preposterous nonsense at once!"

"Take pity, Dr. Watson," the wavering voice continued, "pity a poor murdered woman—"

"I insist you stop it!" I seized Kleppini by the collar and lifted him to his feet. He blinked his eyes and shook his head as if coming out of a deep sleep.

"What—what's happened here? I've been in a trance!"

"You know perfectly well what's happened," I snapped back. "You have been disgracing the memory of a decent woman, and you have been accusing an innocent man of her murder!"

"Wait"—Kleppini rubbed at his temples—"yes . . . yes, I begin to remember a little. But I assure you, Dr. Watson, whatever the spirits said is true. They do not lie."

"We know the truth! You are breeding superstitious lies, Kleppini! You are a fraud! A fraud!"

"Fraud? You call me a fraud?" I had deliberately touched a sensitive point, recalling Houdini's old humiliation of the inferior magician. "It is you who are the fraud, Dr. Watson! You and Sherlock Holmes both! Why did you come here? Because you think I am involved! Hah! Ridiculous! The great Sherlock Holmes, accusing an honest spiritualist . . it is he who is the fraud! He has failed! Yes! He tries to find the secret papers? He cannot! And why not? Because they have slipped through the fingers of the great Sherlock Holmes. A murderer! Important documents stolen from under the nose of Sherlock Holmes! He has failed Houdini, and he has failed his country, and who knows what will be the result?" Kleppini fell back on the cushions with a malevolent laugh.

"Now see here," I cried, my limbs shaking with rage, "Sherlock Holmes has yet to fail anyone in this case. Harry Houdini will be proven innocent! I will stake my reputation on it just as readily as Holmes has done. And as for my country, she is safe. Even if the papers are never recovered—" I paused, realizing that I was on the point of a dangerous admission, but too caught up in the emotion of the moment to stop myself. "Even if the papers are never recovered, we are none the worse. There is still one document in the government's possession, one document which safeguards against those which were stolen. So long as we have that, England is safe." I threw another handful of coins into the brass cup. "There now, my friend, why don't you look into your own future. I wonder if it is as bright?" I thrust aside the curtain and rushed from the booth.

Cursing myself I hastened to the far end of the pier and stared angrily out over the Channel. Not only had I made a fool of myself, there was little telling what damage I had done to Holmes's investigation. If only I hadn't let my name slip out! If only that old sailor hadn't been so quick to recognize me!

"Dr. Watson," came a voice from behind me. The young girl from the reading had followed me onto the pier. "My young man would like a word with you."

"Really now," I said, considerably exasperated, "simply tell your young man—"

"He is quite insistent. You will find him by the shooting-range."

Very well, I thought to myself as I started off down the

pier, not only had I made a bollix of the confidence Holmes
had placed in me, but now I would no doubt have to fight
a jealous lover for this bloodless schoolgirl. I approached
the shooting-range full of the conviction that whatever became of me was no more than I deserved.

I spotted the young man by his striped jacket, hunched
over a rifle, making short work of a series of china targets.
He was a first-rate shot.

"See here, young man," said I, hoping to appease him.

"In a moment," came the reply, as five more shots found
their targets.

"Nice shooting, sir," said the pitchman, when all the
targets had been broken. "Here's your prize, then."

Acknowledging the pitchman with a nod, the fellow
turned at last to face me. "Here you are, Watson," said
Sherlock Holmes, handing me a large cloth bear.

· XV ·
ON THE BRIGHTON LINE

"HOLMES, this really is too much," I said, as we boarded the train to London. "Your capacity for disguise grows more remarkable all the time."

"Yes, this is rather a good one," he chuckled, leading me into a private compartment in the forward car, "but I wasn't certain just how good until I saw how completely shocked you were to see me."

"It is astonishing! And all the time I sat wondering if that old sailor could be you."

"No, Watson, when you see a man whose hook is of the same length as his hand, you may be sure that it is not the trapping of a disguise."

"But your age, how did you manage to appear so young?"

"Well, as you can see, there was very little of my true self involved." This was true enough, for as he spoke Holmes began to remove layer after layer of make-up, wax, and gauze paddings, all of which contributed in one way or another to his youthful appearance. "And I'm sorry to say that to a gentleman of your advanced years, anyone walking without a pronounced stoop gives the impression of youth."

"I'm afraid that's true," I allowed, "and yet, the disguise fooled the others."

"Actually not, Watson. Deceiving Herr Kleppini was my only concern. The girl and the sailor were in my employ."

"What! Then the sailor's remarks—the girl's attentions towards me—?"

"Fear not, old boy. No doubt the young lady would inevitably have succumbed to your attractions, even without my prodding. As for the sailor, Wooden Jack, yes, his actions were entirely of my own devising. It was necessary that the entire scene be carefully orchestrated beforehand. I thought it played out rather well, don't you?"

"But—I—" Vainly I sought to make sense of what had passed, but I could find no logic to what Holmes was telling me. "You must explain all of this from the beginning," I said. "How did you manage to arrive in Brighton before me? I saw you walk away from the platform, and mine was the last train down this afternoon. Did you hire a special?"

"You might say that," he answered, dabbing at the remaining traces of make-up with a coarse towel. "Now, Watson, we have precisely sixty-seven minutes left before reaching London. I shall endeavour in that time to explain the matter fully." He felt about in his pockets for a pipe, though apparently he had not thought to include one in his commercial traveller's attire. I offered a cigar. "Thank you," he said, leaning back in his seat. "Very well. As you yourself have asserted, Watson, it has become necessary to conclude this investigation as quickly as can be managed. I have hourly wires from Lord O'Neill apprising me of recent Anglo-Germanic communications. They have a grim tenor, Watson, very grim indeed. It is only a question of a day or so before Houdini is thrown to the wolves, merely to appease the High Court of Cologne."

"This is terrible!" I cried.

"Quite," Holmes agreed. "Therefore, a precipitous course of action was indicated. While I would most assuredly have discovered the true particulars of the plot in my own fashion, that may have taken as many as four more days. I find that we do not have that much time."

"That is clear enough," I said, "but I don't see how our

exploit in Brighton can possibly bring about a swifter conclusion to the case."

"My good fellow, the case will be solved by morning!"

"By morning! But how?"

"Allow me," he said, reaching over to pull down the
window coverings which separated our compartment from
the passageway. "We are getting ahead of ourselves. Let us
return to our parting in Victoria. You will recall asking how
I could be so certain that the Gairstowe letters had not
already been applied to whatever blackmail or scandal
motivated their theft. This was an extremely sound question, Watson. I replied that Lord O'Neill had discovered a
letter which discredited the others, shielding the prince
against any foul play."

I recalled with shame how I had blurted out this information to Kleppini, inflicting untold damage upon the careful
plans of Holmes. "I'm terribly sorry, Holmes, I know I
have—"

Holmes held up his hand. "Not a word, Watson. You
must hear all of this." He dabbed at the last remnant of
make-up on his face with a pocket square. "I chose to answer your question by telling you of this letter, and in doing
so I provided a comfortable safeguard against our possible
failure to recover the letters. Had I been telling the truth,
this safeguard would have granted us the leisure to conduct
our investigation properly. As it happens—"

"You lied?"

"Shamefully. There is no such letter at Gairstowe. All of
the papers were stolen, and they could at any moment bring
disgrace and ruin to the future sovereign of England."

"This is horrible!" I cried. "But if this is the case, what
was the purpose of telling me otherwise?"

"So that you would believe it to be true."

"Holmes, don't talk in circles! If I have been deceived I
deserve an explanation!"

"I am trying to provide one," he said quietly. "I wished

you to believe that this document existed so that you would tell as much to Kleppini."

"Then . . . then . . ." At last I began to perceive that I had been the unwitting object of an exceedingly devious manipulation. "How could you have known that I would divulge the information to Kleppini? I am not by nature a gossip."

"No, you are not," Holmes agreed. "But from the moment you entered Kleppini's booth, every word uttered by myself, the girl, and Wooden Jack was calculated to produce your outburst."

"You—then all of the indignities I have borne were contrivances of your own?"

"Yes," Holmes said with a merry chuckle. "You must forgive me, but it really is quite amusing. I knew that only an extreme personal affront would cause you to betray my confidence, and the simplest way to affront you proved to be a test of your loyalty to me!" He sank back against the seat, laughing heartily. "Quite ironic, is it not?"

I regarded him for some moments in cold silence, my anger building as his laughter subsided into a series of contented chuckles. "Holmes," I said at length, "I do not see the mirth in all this. You have flouted my loyalty to you, engineered a public humiliation, and what is more, you seem to find all of it marvellously entertaining!"

"My dear fellow!" cried Holmes, seeing at last that I was deeply offended. "Pray forgive me! I assumed that you would understand, once you saw how—"

"I understand nothing," I returned, cutting short his excuses, "save that my feelings are beneath your notice. I am less a friend than a chess piece to you, Holmes!"

"Watson—!"

"If you had wanted Kleppini to know about this new letter, you could very simply have told me the truth! I'd have played along with your gambit as well as the girl or the sailor! But instead you chose to make a mockery of my years of faithful companionship!"

"Watson, you must allow me—!"

"I'm having none of it, Holmes!" I shouted, turning away from him to control my outburst. "Do not try to explain," I said, composing myself with great effort. "The facts are plain enough. I see that our association is no longer of use to you, Holmes. Perhaps I had best end it here."

Seldom have any words of mine produced such a marked effect on Sherlock Holmes. He could not have seemed more shocked if I had threatened to throw him off the train. In truth, his surprise and apparent contrition caused me a great deal of satisfaction, but for the time I contented myself to look stoically out of our compartment window, leaving him to his thoughts.

How long we sat in silence I cannot say, but when Holmes spoke again his jocular tone had been entirely replaced by one of earnest conviction. "Watson," he said, not meeting my eye, "for more than twenty years I have been honoured by your friendship, yet in all that time I can recall little which I have done to earn it. Having few emotions myself, I tend to disregard those of others, save as a means to a logical end. My deception this afternoon was just such a means, Watson. Yes, it is true that I took the girl and Wooden Jack into my confidence, but the burden of convincing Kleppini of the new letter did not rest with them, it rested with you. You are not an actor, Watson. I required that your conviction be fueled by actual belief. That is why I misled you. In doing so I have wounded you deeply. I can do nothing more than offer my apologies. Once the case is solved and the full implication of what I have done is known to you, I am sure you will forgive me."

"Meaning to say that I deserve no further explanation until then?"

"I have no explanation to give! The case is not yet solved!"

"But surely you have a theory?"

"It is pure speculation. As you have often heard me say,

it is a capital mistake to theorize in advance of the facts. This case is such that I haven't had time to gather all of the facts. Accordingly, I was forced to take the measures which you have found so offensive."

"But what good will come of it? You must tell me that much."

"Very well," he said with a sigh, "I shall try to explain everything so far as I have determined, but you shall have to forgive me where I will inevitably be proven wrong."

"I shall bear that in mind for posterity," I said drily.

"I'm certain that you shall," Holmes said. "Now, you recall that when I asked you to come to Brighton it was to observe whether or not a substitute could have taken Kleppini's place at one of his seances, allowing the real Kleppini time to return from London before he was missed."

"But this was a ruse to cause me to reveal the existence of the safeguard letter."

"Actually, I had both aims in mind. And now that you have attended Kleppini's reading, what do you conclude about the man himself?"

"Well," I began, recalling what I had supposed was the purpose of my journey to Brighton, "I saw nothing at the reading that bespoke any great skill or talent."

"Precisely so," Holmes agreed.

"Though I didn't see him attempt any conjuring tricks or escapes, his manner hardly supports the notion that he is a serious rival of Houdini."

"I entirely agree. The man is no match for Houdini. Which leads me to wonder how he can so very nearly be a match for me!"

"What can you mean?"

"The problem before us is as subtle and carefully devised as any I have seen. I've not encountered such a devious turn of mind since the death of the professor. I cannot believe that Herr Kleppini is capable of such a crime."

"What? Then you do not believe that Kleppini is the villain?"

"Oh, he is guilty of the theft, surely. And he may have had a hand in the murder. But Kleppini was merely the agent of the crime, not the mind behind it. There is another, much cleverer man at work than he. Someone who has gained cognizance of the daily routine at Gairstowe, and of the peculiar quirks of our new acquaintance Houdini. Our man is capable of planning the inspired breach of the Gairstowe vault, and of the brutal murder of the Countess Valenka. Does that sound to you like Herr Kleppini and his 'spotted lizard of destiny'?"

I agreed that it did not.

"So, there is someone in the shadows, someone who must be brought to light through the series of events which we have just set in motion. By morning we shall have him!"

"So you have said, but I still don't see how our debacle in Brighton can possibly lead to the criminal's capture."

"It will, Watson, it will. First, as soon as we arrive at Victoria, I will go to Baker Street and rid myself of these clothes. You must go directly to Scotland Yard. There you will tell Houdini that the pleasure of his company is requested by Sherlock Holmes."

"But he is locked in a cell!"

"He will not be for long, unless I am very much mistaken. Take these tools, though I doubt he'll need them."

"But Holmes! You did not see him! He was thoroughly bound and chained, even he cannot escape from such restraints!"

"Did he not say that he could?"

"Yes, but—"

"Watson, Houdini may be a braggart, but I do not think he is an idle one."

I thought of Houdini, helpless in his steel and leather cocoon, and prayed that Holmes's confidence would not be disappointed. "Suppose Houdini is able to escape," I asked, "what then?"

"The two of you will meet me at the gate of Gairstowe House. With Houdini's aid, we will break into the Gairstowe vault, just as Kleppini must have done on the night of the crime, and just as he will have to do again this evening."

"Again this evening! What do you mean by that?"

"You yourself have just told Kleppini that a document exists which renders those he stole useless. Even as we speak, he is contacting his mysterious employer with this unsettling bit of information. They will have but one recourse. They will have to steal the document in order to protect their plan."

"But there is no such document!"

"They do not know that."

"I see," I said admiringly. "And when they break in—?"

"We will be waiting."

"Will we get both of them, Kleppini and the mastermind?"

"I believe the theft will require both of them. Perhaps now you understand why it was necessary to deceive you as I did. We are forcing their hand, my friend." Our train thundered across the rail bridge, moments from Victoria. "The final card has now been played. Now, Watson"—his voice was hushed, but his grey eyes gleamed with an inner fire—"now, truly, the game is afoot!"

· XVI ·
HOUDINI UNBOUND

I HAD NO GREAT DIFFICULTY gaining readmittance to the Scotland Yard gaol that evening, nor was the guard at all reluctant to leave me unattended outside of Houdini's cell. "That bloke ain't going nowhere," said the guard with a laugh, leaving us alone in the empty block of cells.

Peering through the small barred window in the door of Houdini's cell, I found the magician bound as securely as ever and looking, if possible, even more dispirited and piteous than when I had left him. His was a face heavy with affliction; but seeing me, the faintest glimmer of hope ignited in his doleful eyes—an unspoken query to which I responded with only the barest nod of my head. Immediately Houdini's face—indeed his very form, trammelled as it was—seemed to flare with energy, as though the very thought of freedom had rekindled his still indomitable spirit. With a grateful sigh, Houdini closed his eyes, tilted his head back in deepest concentration, and there then began the most remarkable sequence of human exertions I have ever witnessed.

I have been told since that I am the only man who ever saw Houdini escape from a prison cell. This is to be regretted, for none of his public feats, remarkable though they were, can have matched the sheer drama and exhilaration of that solitary struggle at Scotland Yard. Thinking on the scene now, I realize that the studied grandeur and careful suspense of Houdini's stage performances were as nothing to the unembellished rigour of the challenges he met alone.

If ever his skill, knowledge, and strength were truly tested in all their individual and collective applications, it was not on some bright stage with his practised mannerisms and gilt properties, but there in that dank, cheerless prison. There he seemed to confront not only his physical constraints, but also the more formidable onus of personal vindication.

It began slowly enough, as Houdini sat straining his shoulders in a rhythmic motion against the layered bonds, the very motion which I had earlier mistaken for an effort to relax his muscles. "I'm trying to get some slack in these straps," he explained. "I don't need much, but it's very difficult. I'm completely wrapped in canvas under all of this. They must have thought the canvas would make it harder on me, but actually it will help me to use the slack I get up here in other places. All I need is to be able to move my arm an inch or two."

"I see," I said, in what I hoped was an encouraging tone, "and this movement will help you obtain that slack?"

"Let's hope so, Doctor," Houdini said with a wan smile, casually up-ending his chair with his feet so that it crashed over with painful force.

"Mr. Houdini!" I cried, gripping the barred window which separated us. "Are you hurt?"

"Not at all, Doctor," said he, still strapped into the chair which now lay on its side. "And please call me Harry."

"And you must call me John," I said, watching with open-mouthed fascination as Houdini's left arm began the most peculiar twists and undulations beneath its heavy bonds.

"If I can—just—slip off this one loop of chain—" Houdini's voice came in taut gasps of effort. "That's all—I need—there!" he cried, as a small section of chain slipped over the arm of the chair. "That's the first step."

"Excellent!" I cried, though exactly what he thought he had gained was not clear to me. The one small loop of chain seemed a rather minute victory in the face of his complete cincture.

"You see, John," Houdini explained, his head resting on the floor, "my legs are absolutely immobile. But I've given myself some slack, just enough so that I might be able to work my foot through some of these chains and straps."

Houdini began to twist and turn his leg, straining against the bonds which held it to the leg of the chair. The movement was so slight and so restricted that it was impossible to detect any progress. "I think—I'm getting some movement," he said through clenched teeth, sweat dampening his brow. "Very—difficult, though."

I watched in horror as a steel chain drawn tight about his calf raked his flesh even through the layer of canvas, causing slashes of blood to seep through the material. "Just— a little more," he gasped, fighting back what must have been terrible pain. "There now," came a long sigh. "A moment to regain my strength, and then on to step two."

"What is step two?" I asked, a little fearfully. Houdini did not reply. Again he closed his eyes, and then, with a desperate, convulsive strength, he began to buck and strain at the chair itself, trying, hopelessly, it appeared, to wrench his body into a tight ball even against the bonds which held him. It seemed to me that Houdini was determined to burst the constraints by sheer force of his muscles. On and on he strained, with a violence that rent the very air about him, until, with a crack that was barely audible above the groans of his labours, one leg of the chair gave way, allowing Houdini a precious bit of leverage. With a massive, final effort, Houdini twisted his body double, splintering the heavy wooden chair into a dozen fragments.

Free of the chair, but still completely ensconsed in the bindings, Houdini lay so still among the wooden shards that I worried the effort had killed him.

"Houdini—?" I asked tentatively. "Harry? Are you all right?"

"Perfectly fine," he replied brightly, his energy miraculously restored, "and now, step three."

Looking very much like a lively Egyptian mummy, Houdini rolled away from the remains of the chair which had held him and lay flat on the cold stone floor of his cell. Only the outermost layer of his shroud had been loosened as he broke away from the chair. He was still wrapped as tightly as ever in a seemingly impregnable thickness of fetters. Separated from him by the sturdy door and steel bars, I could only watch helplessly as Houdini began his struggle anew. I daresay I felt the torment almost as keenly as he did when, with redoubled effort, Houdini writhed and groaned, rolled and kicked, so that in all ways his condition now resembled that of a madman. Perhaps that is what so frightened me; the recognition that I had seen a somewhat similar struggle before, years earlier, when I had watched a patient at Bedlam in his death throes.

So far as I was able, I tried to determine Houdini's progress by the positions of his arms and legs within the confining cocoon, but this soon proved impossible. So laborious were his efforts that I found myself arriving at the absurd conclusion that he must have four arms and three legs at work under all that leather and steel. At one point, though, I could not fail to observe a hideous protrusion just below his neck, which, even amid all of his other contortions, indicated a serious injury.

"Houdini!" I cried. "Your shoulder is dislocated!"

"I know—" he gasped, mastering the discomfort with short swallows of air. "Did it—intentionally."

"But the pain! It must be excrutiating!"

"Not—so bad." He choked. "It—it's necessary to bring —arm about—there!" He expelled a long breath. "It's back in the socket, and my hand is where I need it."

Indeed, for the first time a bit of Houdini's body became visible as his hand inched upward along his neck, pulling free of the thick leather collar and chains. Even for all I had seen, it was not until that hand appeared that I fully realized there was a method to all this madness, and that the great escape artist actually would be able to escape. This realization so gladdened my heart that I was unable to stop myself from cheering and pounding gleefully on the door of the cell. "Bravo!" I shouted. "Bravo, Houdini!"

"Calm down, John," Houdini cautioned from the floor. "Don't bring the guard, I'm not out yet. This is only step four." It occurred to me then that these careful steps and progressions of his were rather like the methods of Sherlock Holmes, in which a seemingly impossible problem was solved through a meticulously planned and flawlessly executed series of stratagems. While Holmes's exertions were primarily cerebral, Houdini's possessed an almost identical artistic cunning which, as I watched him unfasten a heavy steel clasp about his throat, seemed no less incredible.

"That first buckle was the hardest," Houdini said, straining his free hand toward the next in a line which held the leather straps about him. "Now I should be able to get the second—there—and the third—" But despite his best effort, Houdini was unable to reach the third buckle with his free hand. Undaunted, he bent his body double and seized the buckle in his teeth, pulling it open with a brisk snap of his head.

"Bravo!" I cried again, being careful this time not to rouse the guard. "I've never seen anything like it!"

"I'd be surprised if you had," Houdini answered with a laugh. "No one else can do it!" With this deserved self-flattery, Houdini undertook what was plainly the last in his series of toils. Twisting and turning still more, ever loosening the swathe about him, Houdini at last began to writhe free of the formidable bonds. Inch by inch, first his arm, then his shoulder, Houdini undulated towards his freedom. At first I was irresistibly reminded of a butterfly emerging from its cocoon. But as Houdini progressed, the impression became that of a babe at birth, a notion given weight by the unexplained absence of his clothing, and, even more distressingly, by the raw and bloodied condition of his exposed flesh.

"Harry!" I cried. "You are badly hurt!"

"It's nothing, Doctor," he assured me.

"Nothing? You are bleeding! And where are your clothes?"

"They took them away from me before I was tied up," he answered, now half free of the swaddling, "in case I had any tools concealed in them."

"Abominable!"

"Not really, John. I do have tools concealed in them."

"But it is an insult! You have been seriously degraded!"

"Perhaps," said he, casting off the last of those ungodly bonds with an exhausted but triumphant gesture, "but not any longer. Now I am a free man."

It is impossible to say who felt the greater sense of relief as Houdini lay back on the cold stone floor of his cell. He had just overcome what may well have been the greatest single challenge of his career; but I, still clutching at that small barred window, felt tremendously moved as though I, too, had undergone an arduous rite, and I found myself offering a silent prayer of thanks.

At length Houdini drew himself up, stretching and testing his sore limbs, and examined his surroundings as if for the first time. "Well, my friend," he said, pacing about the cell, "I'd say the first thing we have to do is to recover my clothes. They're in a cell at the end of the corridor."

"Have you forgotten that you are still locked in a prison cell?" I asked. "The first thing we must do is to get you out of there. I have brought Holmes's lock-picking tools, will they be sufficient for you to—?"

It was over in an instant—a flash of metal, a sharp click, Houdini's hand rapping against the lock-plate—and the heavy cell door swung open, before I had even managed to complete my sentence.

"Were you saying something, John?"

"I thought your tools were in your clothes," I replied evenly.

"Only some of them, John. Only some of them." He gave me his trademark wink. "Hmm. These British gaols are a bit draughty. We must find my clothes before I catch pneumonia."

"Very good. And then we must find a way to get you out of this building. My plan is this: I shall go to the main entrance and distract the guards in some manner, enabling you to—"

"No, John."

"What do you mean? It may be a bit risky, but surely—"

"No, no. You don't understand. I won't let you compromise yourself any further on my behalf. You are already implicated in my escape. If it becomes known that you have helped me in any way, you would be considered as guilty as I am."

"I assure you, I am fully aware of the indelicacy of the situation, but it is still my full wish to assist you. Nothing would give me greater pleasure."

"I thank you for that, John. You are a true gentleman. But I can get out of here without placing you in the hazard. You have a cab? Good. Pull it around by the west wall, near the exercise yard. I'll get my clothes and join you there in ten minutes. It will be a full two hours before I am missed."

"You're certain you can manage alone?"

"Certain? I am Houdini! Now go and tell the guard I am asleep. Or that I am busy singing British anthems."

"But Harry," I asked as he hastened me off towards the exit, "how is it that you have waited until now to escape, if you were so readily able to do so earlier?"

"Because I gave Holmes my word of honour that I would *not*, and that," he said, swinging the cell door closed, "is the one bond I never break."

· XVII ·

VIGIL AT GAIRSTOWE

WITHIN TEN MINUTES Houdini and I were clattering through the night on our way to Stoke Newington. In that short space of time, Houdini had located and donned his black suit, escaped from the prison building, and scaled the wall of the exercise yard. Looking not in the least bit the worse for these efforts, he listened eagerly as I described the events of the previous two days and outlined our purpose in returning to Gairstowe House.

"I see you had much the same reaction as I did to Herr Kleppini," Houdini commented when I had finished. "Likeable fellow, isn't he?"

"He is a villain, just as you said; and if Holmes is correct, Kleppini will not be the only one we capture this evening."

"Yes, a mysterious stranger. I wonder who it could be?"

"I'm sure I don't know, though I fancy Holmes suspects more than he was telling."

"Possibly, but don't blame him for keeping it from you, John. We all have our professional secrets. They provide a useful distraction from our private ones."

I was curious to know just what he meant by this remark, but I did not press the point for we had arrived at the wrought-iron gates of Gairstowe House. Stepping down from the cab, I was surprised to see young Turks, the amiable guard I had met previously, standing at the sentry-post.

"Dr. Watson!" he called. "There you are! I've had a wire from Lord O'Neill asking me to take the late watch this evening. He seemed to feel that you might need me."

"Very good," I said. "Thank you."

"Not at all. Nasty night, though," he said, fortifying himself with the contents of a small flask. "Very nasty night."

Turks's assessment was correct. A heavy fog now lent a chill to an already bitter night. Houdini did not have an overcoat, but he did not appear affected by the cold.

"This fog is just as eerie as I'd imagined," he said, peering about. "I've read about London fogs in . . . well, in your stories, John. All that's missing now is—"

From out of the swirling mists stepped Sherlock Holmes, dressed in his inverness travelling cape and deerstalker cap.

"Good evening, Watson," said he. "Ready for the hunt? Mr. Houdini, I am delighted that you could join us."

"Nothing could have kept me away."

"I thought not. Turks, you'd best remain at your post. And mind our horses and trap, if you would. Now, gentlemen, shall we go in?"

Turks swung open the gate and the three of us proceeded to the marbled entrance. "We'd better not use any of the interior lighting," Holmes cautioned. "I have brought the dark lantern; it should suffice." He reached under his cloak and withdrew not only the lantern, but also my service revolver, which he handed to me without comment.

"Expecting trouble?" Houdini raised his eyebrows at this.

"Watson's revolver often takes up where deductive reasoning leaves off," Holmes answered, guiding us down the dim passageway which led to Lord O'Neill's study. "Here we are," he said, shining the lantern on the massive vault door, which was now securely closed. "This is the room from which you are supposed to have stolen the papers, Mr. Houdini. If all goes according to design, the real culprits will have to repeat the theft tonight."

"Shall we wait for them here?" I asked.

Holmes cast the lantern's beam about the stark corridor. "There is no cover here," he said. "If we intend to surprise them in the act, we shall have to wait inside the chamber. That is why we have invited Mr. Houdini. Now, if you would be so good as to open the vault door—?"

Houdini eyed the vault warily and fingered the first of the three complicated locking mechanisms. "Sorry," he said, "I can't do it."

"Houdini," said Holmes impatiently, "this is no time for your professional secrecy. Watson and I will keep quiet."

"You don't understand. I can't do it. I can't get in. I wish I could help you."

"What! But at your performances at the Savoy you open a vault door without so much as blinking an eye!"

"There's a crucial difference, Holmes. At the Savoy I break *out* of a safe. That is a fairly simple thing to do. A safe is designed to keep burglars from breaking in, not from breaking out. Once inside the safe, it is easy to get at the locking mechanisms. But from the outside, the locks are sealed in metal. I can't get at them."

"This is very inconvenient," Holmes said.

"But Holmes," I offered, "I don't understand why it is necessary for Houdini to open the door at all. Why do we not simply telephone Lord O'Neill and ask him to open the door for us?"

"Because he would never agree to it," Holmes answered quietly.

"I don't understand; I thought he instructed the guard to let us in?"

"Lord O'Neill does not know that we are here. I sent the instructions to Turks in his name."

Houdini laughed. "Looks as if we've both overstepped our limits a bit, eh Holmes? Maybe you're not as clever as Watson makes you out to be."

Eager to prevent what would surely have been an acerbic reply, I unfolded Holmes's elaborate set of lock-picking tools and offered it to Houdini. "Do you suppose these tools might help you to get into the vault? Kleppini must have used a similar set."

"No, my friend. Those tools are useless. They are child's playthings, I'm surprised that a man of your intelligence would be carrying them." I stole a glance at Holmes, but he did not appear to have heard. "I hate to spoil the plan, but there is no possible way for me to get us in there. This is not something I admit lightly."

As Houdini spoke, I perceived a subtle change in the manner of Sherlock Holmes. Despite the apparent frustration of his plan, Holmes had resumed that lightness of spirit which I have come to associate with moments of revelation. Lost in thought, he walked to the vault door and ran his hand along its workings. "Of course," he murmured. "Ingenious." He turned to face us. "I believe that you are right, Houdini. Perhaps I am not so clever, after all. I have certainly not demonstrated any particular skill in this investigation, at any rate. I attribute my failings, at least partially, to the undue haste dictated by circumstance. But now the matter has become plain."

"You have solved the case, Holmes?"

"I know how the robbery was done, Watson. That should occupy us for the present."

"Then you know how Kleppini was able to break into the vault when Houdini could not?" I regretted saying this immediately, for Houdini gave me a murderous look.

"I know how Kleppini got inside the vault, yes."

"Look, Holmes," said Houdini, quite hotly, "I don't know what you're getting at here, but it isn't possible that Kleppini could open that door. I'd stake my last dollar on it."

"You're certain? Then how were the papers stolen?"

"Holmes, Houdini has repeatedly said that the door is impenetrable. If a man of his skills cannot find a way of entering the chamber, surely Kleppini would be far less likely to succeed?" I said this hoping both to appease Houdini and draw out Holmes. Did ever a physician minister to two such sensitive vanities?

"And yet the papers are missing," Holmes reminded us.

Houdini snorted. "Next you'll be telling us that Kleppini converted his body to ectoplasm and oozed through the door! Spit it out, Holmes! How was the crime done?"

"You yourself have given me the answer, Mr. Houdini. Let us redirect your energies to the problem. Now, you are a magician of some repute—"

"World's greatest," Houdini amended quietly.

"Are you? I've heard good reports of T. Nelson Downs, the coin manipulator—"

"I am unquestionably the world's greatest magician and escape artist."

"Fine. Then the question at hand should present little difficulty. Suppose you wished to achieve the illusion of having breached this chamber, but recognized that the door was impassable. How would you go about it?"

"I'd conceal myself inside the room while the vault door was open. That way I could break out from inside once the chamber had been sealed."

"Just so."

"Holmes, do you mean to say that Kleppini was in the room the whole time?" The idea seemed absurd to me. "Even during Lord O'Neill's conference with the prince?"

"Precisely."

Houdini and I stared at the heavy vault door.

"But—"

"That would mean—"

"So it would. If Kleppini has successfully duplicated the crime this evening, he is in the chamber even as we speak."

"But that cannot be!" I instinctively lowered my voice so that if Kleppini were present, he would not overhear. "Kleppini could not—"

"There is no need to lower your voice, Watson. The chamber is quite impervious to sound."

"Kleppini cannot be in the vault," I resumed at a normal volume. "We left him in Brighton. It is inconceivable that he could have arrived here so far in advance of us, however he managed to get inside."

"Look, Holmes," Houdini continued, "I don't know Lord O'Neill very well, but he'd have to be a simpleton to take such precautions to secure the study, and then over-look a man hiding in it!"

"Nevertheless," said Holmes, "Kleppini is hidden in the chamber, and it is only a matter of time before he breaks out."

"Do you propose that we simply wait until he does?"

"I don't see that we have any choice."

"This is absurd!" cried Houdini. "Do you really expect us to wait here, maybe all night, on the chance that Kleppini is in there? Why don't we—"

"Harry," I interrupted gently, "I'm certain that Holmes's theory is correct. I suggest we follow his plan."

"But . . . all right, John. If you say so."

While I had succeeded in calming Houdini, Sherlock Holmes observed our apparent intimacy with a vaguely puzzled expression and fell silent.

Making ourselves as comfortable as possible in the stark corridor, we settled in for what promised to be a long vigil. Within half an hour, Houdini had fallen asleep, and I feared that his snores would penetrate even into the sound-proofed chamber. For my own part, I was far too absorbed in the consequence of our watch to think of sleep. If Holmes's suppositions were correct, Herr Kleppini had somehow—in the short time since my hasty departure from his booth—managed to contact his liaison, come up from Brighton to London, regain entrance to Gairstowe House, and conceal himself in Lord O'Neill's study. Was such a thing possible? Could it have been done in such a limited span of time? How did Kleppini get past the guard? How did he enter the study without alerting Lord O'Neill, who must have been present if the door was open? These were but a few of the questions I pondered in those dark hours of the night, as Houdini slumbered on noisily.

This was not the first time I had been awake all night on a watch with Holmes, but time had not inured me to its discomforts. After two hours my limbs had stiffened and my old wound throbbed miserably. No amount of stretching or shifting provided me with any relief. Holmes, conversely, seemed to thrive under such circumstances. Almost immediately he placed himself into that distant, trance-like state, wherein—though he gives the appearance of complete self-absorption—he is in fact sensitive to and alert for the very slightest outside stimuli, which would instantly impel him into action. I have seen Holmes withdraw into this meditative state on many similar occasions and, strangely enough, at the opera. Thus withdrawn, he bore the tedium of our wait far better than I as the long hours of night dragged past.

Just as the first traces of dawn appeared through a distant window, there came the faint sound of metallic tapping, as if some distant blacksmith were hammering at his anvil. Holmes was on his feet instantly.

"That is Kleppini," he said, now finding it expedient to whisper. "He is opening the vault from the inside. Wake Houdini."

But the magician was already awake and alert, having evidently been roused by the sharp clicking of the metal ratchets.

"He's got the back plate off," said Houdini, just as the first of the vault's three large combination dials began to turn, seemingly of its own accord. "He'll have the door open in seconds."

"Amazing," I whispered.

"Child's play," the magician replied, as the second and third dials spun in turn. "Holmes, can I lay first hands on him? He owes me a debt."

"As you wish," said Holmes.

Moving as if operated by spirit hands, the enormous locking handle dipped down, shooting a column of thick bolts. Slowly the heavy door pulled inward on its rails, flooding the dark passageway with uneven light. The figure of Kleppini, stooped and furtive, emerged from the chamber bathed in a corona of shadow and glare. Houdini must have moved with uncommon stealth, for I was unaware that he had left my side until he appeared before Kleppini, his hands folded across his chest, throwing a gratifying fright into the surprised villain.

"Hello, Kleppini," said the American. "Tonight who the fraud is we shall see."

Even in these remarkable circumstances, Houdini's comment so enraged his rival that Kleppini lashed out with all his strength, striking Houdini in the stomach. As before, on the stage of the Savoy, the powerful blow had no discernible effect on Houdini. Again, the young magician simply smiled, spread his arms, and asked, "Would you care to try again?"

Kleppini seemed inclined to do just that until Holmes and I stepped forward, I with my revolver drawn, to show that further resistance was futile.

"Really, Harry," I said, as he prepared to lock one of his own heavy pairs of handcuffs on Kleppini's wrists, "you ought to be more careful about those blows to the abdomen. They'll get you in trouble one day."

"Oh, come now, Doctor. I'm a man of—"

To this day I am not certain what possessed me to look over my shoulder at that precise moment. Perhaps I heard a sound, or perhaps I saw another presence register in

Kleppini's eyes, but turning about I glimpsed a shadowy figure moving towards us. In its outstretched hand I perceived a menacing glint of steel.

There was no time to shout. Nor can I remember a conscious impulse to take action. I pushed my companions to the ground just as the blue flame of gun-fire darted out from the gloom. I had not moved quickly enough to save myself. I felt a sickening impact in my chest which knocked me to the ground, leaving me but dimly aware of the sound of my own name being shouted as darkness enveloped me.

· XVIII ·
ANOTHER ASTONISHING RECOVERY

I HAVE OFTEN OBSERVED that when the victim of a serious physical trauma regains consciousness, he frequently has difficulty recalling who he is and how he came to be injured. In my case, however, there was no such lapse of memory, for no sooner had I come awake than I became aware of Sherlock Holmes and Harry Houdini, crouched on either side of me, engaged in a strident argument as to whether or not my feet should be elevated.

So, although I had no idea how long I had been unconscious—or indeed how I chanced to have regained consciousness at all—I knew immediately that I was still lying in the corridor outside of Lord O'Neill's study, and I knew also that I had been the recipient of a bullet to the chest. Curiously, I felt none the worse for this.

"You don't understand, Holmes," Houdini was saying, "Mama always said that when someone takes a faint—look Holmes! He's coming around! He's all right!"

"The bullet . . ." I croaked feebly, feeling some pain in my chest as I spoke. "I was shot. . . ."

"Yes, you were, Doctor," said Houdini gravely, "and you should be dead. Stepping in front of bullets is risky stuff. I lost a good friend that way. I'd hate to lose another."*

"I don't follow you. . . . I was shot . . . ?"

*Houdini may be referring to Chung Ling Soo, the oriental conjuror (actually an American) who was shot to death while performing his famous bullet-catching trick.

155

"Here, I'll show you," said the conjuror, patting me on the shoulder. "This is what saved your life." He held up what was left of the kit of lock-picking tools I had been carrying. It looked like a sprung mantel-clock: Twisted metal tools protruded at wild angles from its burst leather folds. Several of the tools clattered to the floor as Houdini unfolded the kit to show where a small calibre bullet had lodged in a cluster of mutilated instruments.

My years with Sherlock Holmes have brought me close to death more times than I can or care to remember, but I don't know that I'd ever had the risks illustrated quite so pointedly.

"I'm a very fortunate man," was all I could manage to say.

"You certainly are," Houdini agreed, examining the tool kit with an odd mixture of wonder and relish. "Hit square in the centre. No wonder the impact knocked you out."

"I'm very fortunate," I echoed stuporously, "very fortunate."

"Yes, I'm glad those tools turned out good for something. But next time try to duck, John. You nearly gave Holmes here a heart failure!"

Holmes did, in fact, look stricken. His face had gone deathly pale, and I have seldom beheld such agitation in his features.

"Watson," he said, clearing his throat uncertainly, "I— I should never have forgiven myself if you had been shot just then. I have grown insensitive to danger, and what is worse, I think nothing of imperilling your life as freely as my own. Perhaps—" he looked away from me, "perhaps you were correct earlier. Perhaps it *would* be best if our association—at least our professional one—were severed."

"Come now, Holmes," I said, painfully drawing myself up into a sitting position, "what I said earlier was said in anger. It was just one of the little emotional outcries which you are so fond of upbraiding me for. And as for the risks attached to your profession, I have always been aware of them. I like to think that my presence in your investigations reduces those dangers somewhat."

"That's certainly true this time, Holmes," Houdini acknowledged. "We might both have bought it if not for the doctor. I see now why he is so valuable to you."

"*In*valuable," Holmes corrected brusquely, and in that moment I forgave him for my humiliation in Brighton.

"Really now, gentlemen," I said, "it's almost as if—my God! Where is Kleppini?"

"He slipped away, of course. That's why you were shot."

"Both of them are gone? How long was I unconscious?"

"Only for a moment, but—Watson! Wait! You are not well enough!" But I was already running down the corridor.

Though my medical instincts warned that I might have cracked a few ribs, I pressed on, ignoring the daggers of pain in my chest. We had come too far, and had far too much at stake to be thwarted by my weakness.

Dawn was already burning off the night fog as I hurried down the marble steps towards the front gates. Holmes and Houdini were at my heels by the time I reached the sentry-post. "Turks!" I cried, trying painfully to catch my breath. "Has anyone passed this way?"

"You mean apart from you gentlemen?"

"Yes, of course! Think, man!"

"Well, the morning staff isn't in yet, so there's only been the milk-delivery cart—"

"The milk cart!" Holmes cried. "Of course! That must be it! Which way did it go?"

"Why, up the road, same as always."

Holmes ran to the centre of the road and threw himself down to examine the tracks. "Ah ha! We may yet catch them! We have two horses to their one! Quick! Our trap is over here!" He leapt up onto the box as Houdini and I scrambled into the back seat. "What an exemplary dolt I've been! I should have guessed the milk cart straight away! That explains those irregular footprints in the study!"

"How?" I asked, but Holmes cracked the reins and I was thrown against the back seat.

Holmes was an accomplished driver of nearly every manner of horse-drawn vehicle, and he soon had our small trap travelling at a speed I wouldn't have dreamed possible. The pursuit took us along a narrow and turning road, making our breakneck pace all the more hazardous. At several bends, our trap careened wildly onto two wheels, but each time Houdini and I managed to throw our weight against the opposite side, bringing us flush once more.

On and on we clattered, tree branches and fence posts flashing past at a dizzying rate, the thundering hooves of the horses throwing up a choking cloud of dirt, until at last we rounded a particularly harrowing turn and caught sight of our quarry some little distance ahead.

Observing our pursuit, the driver of the milk cart whipped more speed out of his horse, but Holmes was rapidly closing the distance between us.

"We've almost got them, Holmes!" Houdini cried excitedly. "Faster! Go faster!"

Holmes shot him a dry look. "Sound thinking," he murmured.

As we drew nearer, I could see two men aboard the milk cart. The driver was Kleppini, and the second, a much larger man, was the mysterious figure who had followed me through Oxford Circus. Then, as before, he had covered his features with a large hat and a long red muffler, making identification impossible even as we pulled to within a few yards of them.

"Stop!" Holmes shouted above the din of the hooves and the clanking of the steel milk canisters. "Don't force us to shoot the horse!"

If the two men heard, they gave no response. Instead, the one in the red muffler crawled into the rear of his cart and seized one of the larger milk canisters. It was clear that he intended to throw it.

"Look out, Holmes!" I cried, "he'll trip our horses!" Holmes pulled up sharply, but it was too late. The can was hurled directly beneath the hooves of our pair. The horses reared up violently, causing our trap to crash over onto its side in a great chaos of cracking wood and panicking horses. Houdini and I were thrown into the brush by the side of the road. Holmes, although he had been pitched forward between the horses, had managed to escape injury by clinging to the wooden cross-harness. Though we were unscathed, the chase was at an end. To add to our frustration, we could see Kleppini waving his hat gleefully as the milk cart sped out of sight.

"Is everyone all right?" asked Holmes, rubbing at his side where, I later learned, he too had cracked a rib. "Watson, you'd best see to the horses."

"They're fine, Holmes. Just shaken is all."

"But this buggy is ruined," Houdini said. "Both axles are broken."

"Then we shall have to continue the pursuit on horseback."

"But surely we've lost them by now?"

"No doubt, but I fancy I know where they are headed." Holmes turned to the escape artist. "Houdini, your Voisin is housed at Ruggles, is it not?"

"How did you know about that?"

"Our elusive friends have been making use of a similar model. That is where they are going now, unless I am very much mistaken. We shall unhitch the horses and take a more direct course across the fields. Then, if you are amenable, we may continue the pursuit from Ruggles."

"This is going to be some chase." Houdini chortled, rubbing his hands together.

"But what is Ruggles?" I asked, as Holmes helped me up onto one of the horses. "What is a Voisin?"

The two ignored my questions. "Well, Houdini?" Holmes prompted, waiting to help Houdini onto a horse.

The young American shuffled his feet uncomfortably. "Uh . . . I've . . . I've never ridden a horse before," he admitted.

"Then you shall be in excellent care with Watson," said Holmes, giving him a leg up behind me. "Simply think of it as an exercise in leverage and balance. Come along, Watson! There isn't a moment to lose!"

Holmes swung himself onto the bare back of the other horse—a white charger—and led us off the road and through a cluster of trees. I did not know where we were headed, but I had more than enough to occupy me as we threaded through the trees and then galloped into a clearing on the other side. Houdini proved an unsteady horseman, given to sudden and awkward shifts of position which threatened to unseat us both. I myself was never much of a bareback rider, so my nervous passenger and painful ribs made matters all the more difficult as I struggled to keep apace with Holmes.

Charging through the early dawn, we seemed distinctly at odds with the peaceful countryside about us. The still blanket of morning seemed to pull back an inch or so as we thundered past, and then close up again behind, leaving no witness to our passing except a young stable boy, who paused in his early chores just long enough to salute.

We were indeed an odd cavalry: Holmes taking the point, his sharp profile jutting out above the noble head of his mount, I urging my horse along behind him, and Houdini continuing his unsettling gyrations at the stern. The path we followed—notable for its disregard of topography—was determined entirely by Holmes's bulldog sense of direction. This led us across streams, up hillsides, over fences and, at one point, through a startled fold of lambs.

Proceeding in this rather frantic manner, it was not long before we caught sight of three large storage barns grouped behind a tall wooden derrick and a short length of railroad track, the purpose of which I could not guess. We made for the barns, though nothing in their appearance enlightened me as to how they would advance our pursuit. Were we changing horses?

"Hurry!" Holmes shouted. "There is the milk cart! We have just missed them!"

Houdini leapt off the back of our mount before I had even slowed, rolling briskly down an incline and dashing towards the nearest of the three barns. Holmes was close behind, and together they pulled back the heavy sliding doors. Bringing my horse to a halt before the opening, I peered uncertainly into the barn.

Though it was then four days since I had met Houdini and our remarkable adventure had begun, nothing in that brief but tumultuous time had prepared me for what lay within the barn. The very sight of it froze the blood in my veins. I looked from the magician to the detective in stark disbelief.

"Yes, Watson," said Sherlock Holmes, "it is a flying machine."

· XIX ·
FLIGHT

READERS OF THE PRESENT DAY may find some amusement in
my fear of aeroplanes. We have now, after all, seen aeroplanes applied to both commercial and military en-
deavours, and their design and capability improve with
each passing year. Why then should a man of science, such
as myself, regard them with such intense trepidation?

Simply put, I have lived the bulk of my life under Victoria,
and in that simpler but by no means unenlightened time,
the idea of flight was considered an impossibility, the fanci-
ful theorizing of undisciplined minds. When, in 1903, the
Wright brothers proved otherwise, there came a grudging
acceptance of the principles of aviation, but also a conviction that flight itself was best left to young daredevils and
fools, preferably those possessed of neither family nor
debts. I am an old man now, and I have seen this phenomenon mature into a commonplace, but I still cannot shake off
the notion that man was never meant to fly.

These sentiments, now given lie by the passing of seventeen years, seemed on that morning to be a question of life
or death. For it was obvious to me, as Holmes and Houdini
pushed the fearsome contraption forward on its bicycle
wheels, that it was their intention to continue our pursuit
of Kleppini in the sky. For me, this prospect held all the
attraction of a visit to hell.

"Holmes, have you abandoned your senses?" I asked as
he and Houdini rolled the aircraft towards the tower con-

struct I had noted earlier. "Houdini, do you seriously propose that we are to soar off into the heavens?" I took a few tentative steps after them. "It is preposterous!"

"Come on, John," Houdini said. "I rode a horse just now, didn't I?"

"It's—it's hardly the same thing!"

"No? Believe me, it'll take more than a can of milk to bring this thing down!" Houdini gave what he meant to be a reassuring laugh and continued pushing the craft towards the tower.

"At least in that case we did not fall very *far* down. But this . . . this . . ." I threw up my hands in despair.

"Look, John, I've flown dozens of times. I broke my arm once, that's all. It's perfectly safe."

"That is of little comfort, coming from a man who routinely imprisons himself in a tank of water." I looked over to where Holmes was pushing the other wing. "How is it that you are a party to this madness, Holmes?"

He glanced over at me. "I've flown myself."

"What?"

"Of course. Houdini, hand me the roller, won't you?" They had by now reached the tall tower, and were pointing the aeroplane down the length of railroad track. As curious as I was about this singular device, I was not to be put off my present line of questioning.

"Holmes, you've flown an aircraft?"

"Several times." He had crawled under the wings of the craft, but he continued to address me as though delivering a university lecture. "The necessity of aeroplane travel became obvious from the moment I began this investigation. Proceeding, as I did, from the assumption that Houdini did not commit the Gairstowe burglary, I had to deal with the problem of Herr Kleppini's apparent ubiquity."

"What does that mean, Holmes?" asked Houdini, who was engaged in some adjustment of the engine.

"It simply means," Holmes continued from beneath the craft, "that Kleppini could not be in Brighton and in London at the same time. So, if he was responsible for the burglary, he could not very well have performed in Brighton that same evening. Yet, my continued inquiries suggested that he had indeed done both things. I was left to conclude that either he had arranged for a substitute to take his place in Brighton, or he had procured a very rapid means of transportation. I quickly discovered that he owned an aeroplane very much like this one."

"Hah!" Houdini snorted. "He was probably jealous of mine!"

"Possibly, or perhaps he recognized the sluggishness of the trains when one must travel from London to Brighton in thirty minutes."

"Good Lord, Holmes! Is the aeroplane really that fast?"

"It is," he said, rolling out from under the wing. "I have done it myself."

"No!"

"You will recall that I placed you on a train in Victoria and yet managed to reach Brighton in advance of you?"

"You flew?"

"Yes. That was my first solo flight. It was positively exhilarating. In fact, you had earlier mistaken my heightened spirits for a return to narcotic use. Terribly mistrustful of you, Doctor."

"My apologies, I'm sure; but you will allow that what is exhilarating to you is madness to me. That you, one of the brightest lights of our era, should risk your life at such—"

"Holmes," Houdini broke in, pointing to the tower, "we'll have to add to the drop-weight if we expect to get off the ground."

"And there's another thing," I cried in exasperation. "What on earth is the purpose of that device?"

"Ah! Allow me to explain," said Houdini, happily assuming Holmes's professorial air. "Like the aeroplane itself, this launching apparatus was designed by the Wright brothers. Americans, you know. The tower you see here hoists this cylinder-weight about forty feet into the air. Then, as it is released, a cable pulls the aeroplane along the railroad track in the opposite direction. The aeroplane gains speed as the weight falls to earth, so that by the time the weight hits the bottom, the 'plane is moving fast enough to leave the ground."

"You make it seem so simple, and yet—"

"The only problem," Houdini continued, thoroughly enjoying his role as lecturer, "is that the drop-weight will have to be made heavier to account for the added weight of you and Holmes."

"If my weight is such a problem, hadn't I best stay on the ground?"

"I'm afraid I'll need you to balance out Holmes. Where is Holmes, anyway? Ah, here he is. He's found some chains. Just what we need."

While the two of them set to wrapping the heavy chains about the drop-weight as Houdini had mentioned, I took the opportunity to examine the aircraft which they so confidently intended to fling into the sky.

The craft was of a stark and spare design, constructed of little more than wooden spars and panels of fabric. While it had two long continuous wings, one above the other, they were quite delicate in appearance and did little to bolster my enthusiasm. Some thirty feet across, the wings were merely concave frames covered with heavy cloth, connected to each other by numerous wooden supports and steel cables which served only to emphasize their fragility.

At the centre of the lower wing was a squat wooden seat for the pilot and an ordinary leather-covered automobile steering-wheel. No other means of controlling the craft were apparent. Behind the seat was a small petrol engine which served to power a large wooden propeller. This propeller, which faced the rear of the craft, stood nearly as tall as a man.

Beyond the propeller extended the tail of the craft, a bare frame of wood and criss-crossed struts which stretched for twenty-five feet or so, finally resolving itself into something like a box kite at the far end.

To the fore of the craft was a short protrusion resembling a whale's tail, which was connected by two thin cables to the steering-wheel.

My scrutiny of the aircraft, brief though it was, did little to enhance my confidence in its function; and indeed it struck me as rather overly ambitious of this ragtag collection of firewood to aspire to flight.

In the meanwhile, Holmes and Houdini had secured the heavy chains about the drop-weight, and were now struggling to hoist the weight to the top of the tower by means of a rope pulley.

"Come and give us a hand, John," Houdini called as he strained against the heavy weight. "This is usually a job for five men."

"But . . . I . . . ." Watching them toil with the pulley, I was reminded of the ancient hoists used to lift knights in armour onto their horses. While this was a pleasant enough association, it is perhaps some measure of my natural disinclination towards modern aviation. A very real and paralysing fear now gripped me, and I believe that Holmes must have sensed my discomfort, for he addressed me quite civilly despite his maddening struggle with the drop-weight.

"Watson," he said, pulling fiercely on the rope, "within the last five minutes our quarry departed in an aircraft very similar to this one. They will head directly for the Channel. If they manage to leave the country, England will never see King George V." He gave another pull at the rope. "Therefore, I would be very much obliged if you would help us to pull up this weight."

With a sigh of resignation, I stepped over to the tower and took my place beside them. "All right, gentlemen," said I, grasping the rope firmly. "Pull!"

After a brief but rigorous struggle, we managed to hoist the drop-weight up to the top of the tower, where Houdini secured it with a locking lever.

"All right then!" the magician cried. "We're ready to go! John, you and Holmes will have to lie flush across the wings on either side of me. Better balance that way."

"Harry . . . are you sure . . . ?"

"She's really something, isn't she?" He gestured to a panel of fabric upon which his name was printed in bold letters. "Long after the world has forgotten Houdini the magician, they will remember Houdini the aviator!"

"I only hope she's as fast as you say," Holmes commented. "Kleppini is flying a slower model, but we've given him nearly five minutes of advantage."

"That's nothing!" Houdini scoffed. "We'll make it up easy. Come on, John. Up you go." He stood ready to help me up onto the wing.

"I'm expected simply to drape myself over the wing? I'll fall off!"

"No you won't," he assured me, "as long as you lie in close to the cockpit you'll be protected from the wind. That's called the dead space."

"Delightful."

"Look, if you'll feel better, here's something to hang on to." He snapped a pair of handcuffs onto one of the wing spars. "You can get a good grip on that. Now let's be off."

"All right," I sighed, climbing onto the lower wing and trying to lay myself as flat across its width as possible. Like a child regretting a foolish dare, I gripped my supports and waited.

Houdini leapt into the pilot's seat and gave a signal to Holmes, who spun the huge propeller. The engine started up immediately and the propeller began to turn faster and faster, making an insufferable racket as Holmes climbed onto the other side of the wing. We were now ready for flight.

Pulling on a leather cap and goggles, Houdini turned to say something to me which was drowned out by the sound of the engine. Seeing that I had not heard, he simply gave a jaunty thumbs-up signal and pulled the cord which released the drop-weight.

The aeroplane shot forward along the track, bouncing and quaking terrifically as we were thrust towards a grove of trees at the far end of the field. The distance of railroad track cannot have been more than seventy feet, but it might as well have been one hundred miles, for every inch was a torment of buffeting which threatened to shake us loose of the craft. My injured ribs were afire as the very wing upon which I was perched began to bounce up and down alarmingly, and I feared that my ribs or the wing must break at any instant.

Just when it seemed that we would either wrench ourselves apart or crash into the onrushing trees, there came a final, jarring thump, and then all of the jostling was replaced by the steady vibration of the engine.

In that moment we were airborne, and in that same moment I had the queer sensation that all the fluid in my body was being drawn out through the heels. I might well have fainted if not for the strong rush of air across my face. Houdini angled the craft sharply upward, narrowly missing the grove of trees at the end of the field, while I wrapped my arms more securely about the wooden cross-spars and pondered locking myself into the handcuffs.

Only when Houdini brought the aeroplane level, some three hundred feet above the earth, did I summon the courage to look over the front edge of the wing. It was a remarkable sight, a vertical landscape in which tall trees took on the aspect of shrubbery, buildings were like footstools, and all movement took on the distant insignificance of raindrops running down a pane.

Perhaps I was made giddy by the purer air, but my fascination with this aerial sightseeing so absorbed me that it pushed all thoughts of danger and pursuit from my mind. Indeed, in a few more moments I might have become a flying enthusiast if Houdini's excited shouts had not broken my enchantment.

"There they are!" Houdini roared, straining to be heard above the engine. "Their 'plane isn't nearly as fast! We'll catch them in no time at all!"

The other aircraft, roughly four hundred yards distant, looked like some sort of great gliding pterodactyl. Apart from a perceptible quivering of its wings, Kleppini's craft looked positively serene, and I wondered if ours—noisy and tremulous as it was—would appear as majestic when seen from their vantage.

"What did you say, Holmes?" Houdini shouted, pulling off his leather helmet. Whatever Holmes had said was lost to me in the rush of wind and the din of the engine, but Houdini was closer to him and was evidently better able to pick it out.

"I know," Houdini responded as Holmes repeated himself, "but outrunning them isn't good enough! We must find a way to stop them!" He peered off towards the other aircraft. "Maybe we should have left Watson behind after all, we're too heavy for any maneuvering . . . wait!" he cried, suddenly struck with an inspiration. "Can you really fly this thing, Holmes?"

Holmes made a reply, and though I still could not hear, I suspect it was indignant.

"Then come up here and take the control," Houdini

shouted. "Remember, pull in and out to work the elevator, turn the wheel for the rudder. Come on! Change places with me!"

"Wait!" I shouted. "Don't! The wind will carry you to your death!" Holmes could not hear me, though I doubt he would have heeded my warning if he had. Limited as my understanding of our craft was, I knew enough to realize that once Holmes left the sheltering dead space of the wing, he laid himself bare to the very forces which kept the plane aloft. I doubted that even he could long withstand them.

Taking hold of two of the wooden spars, Holmes slowly pulled himself to a standing position on the lower wing. The wind blasted through the folds of his cloak, carrying his deerstalker cap over the edge of the wing. The journey from where he stood to the control was one of only four steps, but each of those steps was a peril of unsteady footing and savage wind, threatening at every moment to carry him overboard. Tentatively making his way inch by inch, hand-hold by handhold, Holmes managed at length to lay hands on the wheel and lower himself into Houdini's seat, while the young magician slipped out beneath and took his place on the exposed wing.

Very little would have surprised me at this point, for I was well convinced that the pair of them had gone insane, but even so I could make no sense of it as Houdini busily fastened a length of rope to two of the sturdier cross-spars. What could he be planning?

Holmes's newly acquired aviation skills served him well as he pointed our craft directly towards Kleppini's and began to overtake it. At the same time, Houdini had lashed his own ankles together with the other end of the rope and, heedless of this impediment, was crawling out to the front edge of the wing on his hands and knees. Despite the dubious precaution of the rope, I feared at every instant that Houdini would be swept off the wing, and twice he was forced to flatten himself against the surface as a particularly bitter gust tore across him. Still he worked doggedly, carrying the rope along the cross-spars for a purpose I could not yet fathom.

We were by now flying directly over Kleppini's aircraft, and it was then that Houdini performed one of those rare acts of bravery which, even as it inspires admiration, raises the dark spectre of the Juggernaut. For Houdini rolled his body to the extreme forward edge of the wing, carefully tested the rope about his ankles, and then gently lowered himself off the wing and into empty space.

Supported only by the one strand of rope around his feet, Houdini spun and swayed like a child's toy head down in the wind. Undaunted, he lowered himself still further, his body bent double to work hand over hand along the rope. This was the attitude he had devised for his open-air straitjacket escapes, but I fancy that even that ordeal was pale compared to this. Dangling like a fish on a hook, he might at any moment break free and plummet to the far distant earth.

Holmes was doing his best to compensate for our now wildly uneven distribution of weight, but even so our craft was listing forward dangerously, so that I had to brace myself more firmly against the supports or be spilled forward off the wing. The forward tilt of the aeroplane left me only too well situated to see that Houdini was now trying to swing himself towards the wing of the craft below. This proved nearly impossible, for though the two aeroplanes were flying almost parallel, Houdini had to contend not only with the violent wind, but also with the unsteady dips and waverings of our imbalanced craft.

After several maddeningly near misses, Houdini did at last manage to grab hold of the extreme lower edge of Kleppini's wing. Working with a strength born of desperation, Houdini pulled himself in under the wing and began tearing away at the fabric beneath. It was clear that, like punching a hole in a child's kite, Houdini intended to cripple the aircraft by ripping through its wing. Of necessity, Houdini was completely taken up with his precarious task, which left him oblivious to a new and more menacing danger.

Though Kleppini was occupied in flying his aircraft, the large man in the red muffler, our mysterious foe, had spotted Houdini and was inching his way along the wing towards him. I was certain that if he reached the spot where Houdini hung by the slender cord, my friend's life would be forfeit.

I shouted to Holmes, but he could not hear me, and evidently he was so busy trying to keep our aeroplane level that he had not observed the new danger.

In times of extreme stress, a man's mind makes peculiar leaps. No sooner had I perceived this new threat to Houdini than I found myself doing precisely what I had thought so parlous only moments before. I released my supports and pulled myself out onto the unsheltered wing of the aeroplane.

I will not pretend that some previously untapped well of bravery guided my actions, for I literally quaked with fear as I crawled forward, the wind tugging at me, my chest on fire, but I knew that I had either to act or watch Houdini be sent to his death some three hundred feet below.

Gripping the edge of the wing with one hand, I aimed my revolver as best I could with the other. The man in the red muffler had nearly reached Houdini by now, but the American, still clinging to the underside of the bottom wing, could not even see his attacker crawling along the top.

Both aeroplanes were now dipping and swaying wildly from imbalance, making careful aim impossible, but as the big man brandished a hunting knife within inches of Houdini's lifeline, I steadied and fired.

My bullet did not find its mark, but it must have passed close enough to alarm Houdini's attacker, for he whirled about, grasping inside his coat for his own revolver. This action proved unwise, for as he took his hand from the support he was shunted over the edge of the inclined wing.

I shall never forget how he clawed at the air as he fell, how his legs thrashed in the empty space; but soon he was beyond sight, beyond sound, and beyond help.

· XX ·

A SLEIGHT UNSEEN

IN THE MOST EXTRAORDINARY WAY, the unfortunate death of the man in the red muffler would soon lead to the successful resolution of our case. If not for his demise, and at precisely the moment and manner in which it occurred, we may never have recovered the Gairstowe letters. This fact, however, was not immediately apparent. My first impression, directly following the hideous incident, was that all of our efforts had been in vain.

We had found it necessary to reduce our speed while Houdini pulled himself back up the rope and onto the wing of our craft. In so doing, we lost sight of Kleppini's aeroplane. Having thus broken off the pursuit, we attempted to recover the remains of Houdini's assailant, but several low passes over the meadow where he had fallen failed to produce any sign of the body. Though he had most assuredly been crushed to death upon impact, all traces were obscured by the tall grass.

"Well, I guess that's it," Houdini said despondently when we had landed the craft at Ruggles (an experience I hope never to repeat!). "We've lost Kleppini, and we can't even find the other fellow's body. I guess we've lost the game."

"On the contrary," said Sherlock Holmes, "our fortunes have taken a decided turn for the better."

"Come on, Holmes," said Houdini, "why don't you face the truth? It's over!"

In the face of what had just occurred, it is easy to see why Houdini became so dispirited, but I knew Holmes far too well to discount his seemingly ungrounded optimism.

"How can our situation have improved, Holmes?" I asked.

"It's quite simple," he began, "with the death of—"

"Oh stop it, Holmes!" Houdini cried angrily. "What's the point of drawing it out? Kleppini is long gone! There's nothing more we can do!"

Sherlock Holmes has had more than his share of doubters over the years, and it is always something of a treat to see how he manages them. I recall one occasion, many years earlier, when he had been called upon to solve the insidious Joruel Strangulations case, a mystery which hinged upon the unexplained disappearance of the murder weapon. "How is it possible for a garotte to vanish into thin air?" Inspector Gregson had demanded. "Explain that, Mr. Sherlock Holmes, and you'll have solved the case!" With a peculiar smile upon his lips, Holmes withdrew a similar garotte from his pocket, exhibited it to Gregson and, without further comment, swallowed it.

The same smile spread across his face now as Holmes stepped to the storage barn and began pushing back the sliding door. He had barely opened it a foot when one of our two horses pushed its way out into the field.

"That's odd," I said. "Where is our other horse?"

"This barn has a back door," Houdini said. "Maybe—good Lord! It can't be!"

Now it was Houdini's turn to be astonished by the contents of the barn, for Holmes had now pushed the door completely open to reveal Herr Kleppini's flying machine.

"Kleppini's 'plane!" Houdini marvelled. "What's it doing here? Why did he come back?"

"Obviously something occurred during the flight which caused him to change his mind about leaving the country.

I think we are on safe ground—in a manner of speaking—to assume that this occurrence was the death of his employer."

"Why should the death of the other man cause Kleppini to return here?" I asked.

"Why indeed? Here, Watson, we enter the heady sphere of deductive reasoning. What would cause Kleppini to arrest his own successful flight?"

"Holmes, is this leading us anywhere?" Houdini demanded, shifting uneasily from foot to foot. "If Kleppini is still in England somewhere, shouldn't we be chasing him?"

"I thought it might be useful if we decided where to look."

"All right, go on."

"Early this morning," Holmes began, as he inspected the damage Houdini had done to the wing of the other craft, "our mysterious adversary arrived at Gairstowe to discover the three of us springing a trap on Kleppini. He very sensibly concluded that his plans had been discovered, and he further realized that the only recourse was to flee the country."

"But what's the point in going over this now?" Houdini asked. "This man, whoever he was, is dead now!"

"Exactly," Holmes agreed, "and with his death, Kleppini suddenly found himself a free agent. No longer bound by his employer's decisions, Kleppini elected, against all logic, to return here. Why? Evidently there is something that the two of them left behind, something which Kleppini believes is worth the considerable risk of capture."

"The Gairstowe papers!"

"Watson, you surpass yourself once more. That was precisely my conclusion."

"Then we must get to Brighton immediately!"

"If the papers were in Brighton, Kleppini would undoubtedly have flown there. The damage to his wing was not great enough to prevent it."

"But . . . then where are they?"

"I believe we shall find Kleppini and the papers at the Savoy."

"My theatre?" cried Houdini. "But why there?"

"I think I know," I said. "You forget that Kleppini's interest in this crime was to create the illusion of your guilt. How better to further that illusion than to place the stolen documents in your possession? That's it, isn't it, Holmes? We must get to the Savoy immediately!"

Sherlock Holmes neither confirmed nor contradicted my conclusion, leaving me with the uneasy feeling that the problem was a good deal more complex than I had divined.

"Look," said he, "here is Kleppini's horse and the milk cart. He must have taken one of our horses, but if we hitch the other to the cart we may yet arrive at the theatre before him."

"One thing bothers me, Holmes," said Houdini. "My assistant Franz spends most of his time at the theatre, and he's always on the look out for intruders."

"We are aware of that," Holmes said ruefully, recalling our last encounter with Franz.

"Well, you've seen what Kleppini is capable of. I'm just afraid that . . . if Franz gets in the way . . ."

"Don't worry," I tried to reassure him, "we'll get there in time."

I must say that neither of us was entirely convinced by my assurances, and Houdini fell grimly silent through the whole of our journey to the Savoy.

With Holmes at the reins we made startlingly good time even when we reached inner-London, for he regarded the congestion of city streets as little more than a mathematical problem. This led to some highly inventive driving techniques, and I doubt that he had endeared himself to the

London traffic constabulary by the time we finally reached the Savoy.

"Look at this!" Houdini snorted, jumping down from the cart before one of his own theatre posters. "It says 'Postponed Indefinitely,' right across my face! I'll demand an official apology before I'm through!"

"There will be time for that later," Holmes said quickly. "I see that Kleppini has already arrived." He pointed to the locks on two of the main doors to the theatre, which bore signs of tampering.

Houdini bent over the locks. "Look at these scratches," he said disdainfully, "and he calls himself an escape artist! I'm surprised he got them open at all! Well, never mind that now—" He withdrew a metal tool and snapped open the doors with two brisk motions. "Hurry! We must see if Franz is all right!"

Holmes took hold of the young magician's arm and pulled him back through the door. "Wait," he said, "we mustn't just charge in, like your President Roosevelt. If we hope to discover where the papers are concealed we must use stealth. I suggest you go around to the stage door and enter through the wings. Watson will go up through the house and I shall search the dressing-rooms."

"We'll sneak up on him, eh? All right, Holmes. Good luck!"

Holmes turned to me as the young American slipped around the side of the building. "Watson, are you quite sure you are able to continue? I observe that you have been favouring your right side."

"So have you," I returned, stepping into the lobby of the theatre. "It appears we have both received injuries."

"That's true," Holmes admitted, rubbing at his own ribs. "Very well, we shall bind up our wounds after the battle. For the time being, stay close to the ground and do not show yourself. Kleppini must be allowed to reveal where he has placed the letters. Work your way down the centre aisle and keep hidden until I call for you. In his desperation to recover the letters, there is no telling what Kleppini might do.''

"But what about Franz? Are we too late to help him?"

"I fear so," said Holmes, vanishing into a corridor which led to the dressing-rooms.

Left alone in the darkened lobby of the theatre, I gathered my resolve and crept to the closed doors of the house itself. Opening one of the doors as silently as possible, I dropped to my hands and knees and crawled into the centre aisle. My attention was immediately drawn to a small figure in the middle of the vast stage, bent over the broken remains of Houdini's Water Torture Cell.

I crept closer, but already I could see that the figure was Kleppini. He was tearing away at the panels of oriental scrollwork about the base of the cell, muttering loud curses as he did so. When this destructive examination did not yield up the letters, Kleppini rose to his feet, gave an angry cry, and toppled the cabinet onto its side. The stage fairly shook as the heavy oaken cabinet fell, shattering its remaining panels of glass and sending bits and shards skittering across the stage.

This ill-treatment of Houdini's prized illusion seemed to give Kleppini a great deal of pleasure, for he stood gloating for a long moment before his eye was drawn to something amid the wreckage.

"Ah ha!" he cried aloud, plucking a bundle of papers from the underside of the cabinet. "I have it!" He eagerly began to untie the ribbon around the packet.

"Dear me!" said Sherlock Holmes, stepping onto the stage. "Look at all of this broken glass! What a mess you've made!"

Kleppini whirled about. "Stay away from me!" he snarled, though his voice betrayed both surprise and fear. "Stay back!"

"Shall I find a push broom?" Holmes asked. "It shouldn't take a moment."

"I'm warning you! Stay back!" The little man fumbled in his pocket and withdrew a long-bladed knife.

"Splendid," said Holmes unconcernedly, "but do promise to straighten up before you leave. After all, it isn't fair that—"

In another moment I'm certain that Holmes would have engineered Kleppini's capture, but at precisely that unfortunate instant, Inspector Lestrade strode blithely across the darkened stage from the opposite side, and before the hapless policeman became aware of the danger, Kleppini had seized him from behind.

"Now you'll have to let me go," Kleppini called, backing Lestrade up to a wall, "or I'll kill this C.I.D. man!"

"I can see that I've come at a bad time—" Lestrade began.

"Quiet!" snapped Kleppini, encircling Lestrade's throat with one arm and drawing the knife close with the other. "Now, Mr. Holmes, don't get any ideas about sneaking up on me!" He looked about nervously, even as I searched frantically for some means of capturing him. "Where is your friend, that Dr. Watson?" Kleppini demanded suspiciously. "And where is Houdini? Answer me!"

Holmes gave a tragic cry and buried his head in his hands. When he looked up a moment later, his eyes were brimming with tears. "All right, then," he cried, his voice quivering, "I can't hide it any longer! Houdini is dead! One of the struts broke as he was climbing back into the aeroplane!"

Holmes was always at ease on the stage, and it was clear that his performance thoroughly convinced not only Kleppini, but Lestrade as well.

"Houdini is dead?" Lestrade repeated. "That's a terrible shame—"

"Quiet!" Kleppini shouted again, tightening his hold around the inspector's neck. "So, he fell out of his 'plane, did he? Good, that saves me a bit of trouble." He took a step away from the wall. "Now if you'll just stand aside, this gentleman and I will be on our way."

All this time I had been looking so desperately for a way to lend assistance that I hadn't noticed Kleppini's grave error. When he had backed Lestrade up to the wall, he had unwittingly chosen the wall used in Houdini's Walking-Through-a-Brick-Wall illusion. This worked very much to our advantage, for as Kleppini took a step away from the wall, Houdini suddenly appeared in the space behind him and brought a heavy vase crashing down on his head. This effectively ended our long pursuit.

This time there had been no screens to shield Houdini's illusion from my eyes, as there had been when we first saw it some days earlier. And while I freely admit that it was very dark in the theatre, and that my line of sight was not ideal, I feel I must record my distinct impression that Houdini passed neither over nor under the solid brick wall, but rather directly through it.

I was still marvelling over this apparent impossibility while Lestrade collected himself and thanked the young magician. "It's a good job you weren't really dead, Mr. Houdini," the inspector said. "I'm certainly in your debt. I can see that Holmes was right about you from the start."

"Thank you, Inspector," Houdini said with a bow. "It was my pleasure to help. Here, you'd better use these hand-cuffs on Kleppini when he wakes up. . . . Oh, on second thought, I guess your cuffs will be good enough for him."

Holmes and I came forward and examined the oblivious figure of Kleppini. "It looks as if you'll have him in a cell by the time he recovers," Holmes said. "But tell me, Lestrade, what brought you down to the Savoy at this hour of the morning?"

"Oh yes, right," Lestrade's face became suddenly grave. "I had come down here to place Mr. Houdini back under arrest, but under the circumstances, we have some bad news." He withdrew a long red muffler from his coat pocket. "It seems your assistant Franz was found dead in the middle of an open field early this morning. He appears to have fallen from a great height. We can't make any sense of it, can you?"

· XXI ·
THE SCIENCE OF DEDUCTION

THE PRINCE OF WALES put a match to the bundle, lit a cigar from the flames, and dropped the burning packet onto a tray. As the paper browned and curled about the royal seal, His Royal Highness sat back in his chair and heaved a sigh of relief.

"I can't tell you what a burden you've lifted from me, Mr. Holmes," he said. "Those letters would have been my ruin. And from what Lord O'Neill tells me, that would have been the least of it."

"That's true," the secretary agreed. "The Germans are ready to seize upon any pretext to increase their hostilities towards us. If those letters had come to light we may never have smoothed it over. As it is, Herr Osey was summoned to Berlin quite abruptly after the murder of the Countess Valenka was discovered. There are troubled times ahead, I'm afraid, but we may be thankful that this incident will not exacerbate them." He paused as the butler wheeled in a tea-trolley and then withdrew. "I've asked you and Dr. Watson to Gairstowe this morning so that you might give us the full details of your investigation. Several points remain unclear."

"Yes," the prince said eagerly, "let's have some tea and you may tell us all about it. I must say I'm full of questions about the case."

Sherlock Holmes rose from his chair as readily as the plaster encasing his ribs would permit. Taking a cup of tea from the trolley, he began to pace the room in a most awkward fashion, teacup in one hand, cane in the other.

"Holmes, hadn't you better sit down?" I asked, for I knew that the plastering of my own ribs had made walking a trial, even with a cane.

"No, Watson. We have been laid by the heels in our rooms for days. This is our first excursion and I intend to stretch myself out a bit. Now then"—he turned to the prince—"I believe that most of the facts are known to you. You must tell me which specific details want clarification."

"Well, for one thing, I've been intrigued as to how the letters were actually taken from this room. We were under the impression that the door is impassable."

"It is," Holmes returned. "Watson and I have that on the very best authority. But as it happened, the door was open when the thief entered the room."

"Impossible!" Lord O'Neill cried. "Unless the countess—?"

"No, not the countess," Holmes answered, trying to hold his saucer and cane in one hand while lifting the teacup to his lips with the other. "Let us think back to my initial examination of this room. You may remember that I was disturbed by the unlikely grouping of footprints found behind the desk. Their origin was also of particular interest to me, as I found that I could not trace the source of the mud."

"Do you mean to say that you know every mud puddle in London?" the prince asked. "I don't believe it!"

"I see that Your Highness had a walk in the Palace gardens this morning," Holmes said quietly. "How are the roses coming on?"

"*Touché!*" the prince cried, waving his cigar. "Do go on."

"While I was examining these footprints, Lord O'Neill became somewhat agitated because there was no milk for the tea."

The secretary gave an embarrassed laugh. "My word, what a memory for detail you have! You can't tell me that milk has any bearing on the theft? It is such an insignificant detail!"

"I was once able to solve a murder by measuring the depth to which the parsley had sunk in the butter on a hot summer day. After that I am hard put to call anything an insignificant detail."

"Your point is taken," Lord O'Neill said, "but how does the lack of milk for my tea relate to the theft?"

"I was struck by the fact that you should run short by mid-morning, when your kitchen staff receives a large delivery at the start of each day. Considering that you had given a reception for the Prince of Wales only one night previously, this oversight seemed all the more unlikely." Having managed to drink his tea while pacing with his cane, Holmes was now endeavouring to fill his pipe. "I began to seek out possible reasons for this shortage," he resumed, ignoring the bits of tobacco which fell in his wake. "But none occurred to me until much later, as we were chasing Franz and Kleppini's milk cart."

"I'm afraid I still don't see exactly how this bears on the crime," I admitted. "Was Franz driving the milk cart during the actual theft?"

"It's very likely," Holmes answered. "You see, it occurred to me as we began to give chase that Kleppini might have been sneaked onto the grounds of the estate concealed in a milk canister. The guards would be so used to receiving milk deliveries that they would be unlikely to open the canisters themselves."

"And that is why Lord O'Neill ran short of milk?"

"Yes. Instead of milk, he had received Kleppini. This answers another of the problems of the case as well. It's clear that at some point prior to reaching the gates of the estate, Franz and Kleppini poured an entire canister of milk onto the ground so that Kleppini could get inside. Having thus created a mud puddle, they took this opportunity to muddy the shoes they had taken from Houdini's dressing-room."

"And that explains why you were unable to identify the mud!" the prince exclaimed. "It was a mixture of milk and earth, not natural mud at all!"

"Precisely."

"So, Kleppini got onto the grounds in a milk canister. How did he manage to break into the vault?"

"Ah, that much should have been plain from the beginning, Sir. On the evening of the theft, the two of you met with Herr Osey and the countess to negotiate the purchase of the letters. It appears that Kleppini was already in the room at that time."

"Impossible!" Lord O'Neill cried. "No one entered the room, and it was locked before we arrived!"

"Earlier you indicated that tea was served."

"Yes, of course, but—"

"Did you recognize the butler?"

"No, he was someone we'd laid on for the reception, but he left promptly."

"Not before he had deposited a visitor."

"What?"

"As the tea-trolley was rolled in, Kleppini was crouched on the lower shelf, hidden from view by the table linen. When the trolley passed behind this sofa, Kleppini quickly stepped out and hid there. There he remained until the four of you had completed your business and left the room, locking him inside with the letters."

"It can't be, Holmes!" Lord O'Neill insisted. "We'd have known if there had been anyone else in the room!"

"It's true," the prince agreed. "What you say is just too fantastic."

"Is it?" came the disembodied voice of Harry Houdini.

"Or is it simply"—he stood up from behind the sofa—"hard to believe?"

Mercifully, I had been forewarned of this dramatic entrance. I had been present as Holmes rehearsed the effect with both Houdini and the butler. Thus, I was able to observe the startled expressions of the prince and Lord O'Neill as Houdini appeared in their midst. Both men were thoroughly astonished, but while the secretary remained so, the prince soon recovered himself and broke into appreciative applause.

"I took the liberty of inviting Mr. Houdini," Holmes said, "because I thought a dramatic illustration of my theory might be in order."

"Mr. Holmes, this is highly irregular," Lord O'Neill said nervously. "We've been discussing extremely sensitive matters—"

"Nonsense!" The prince cried jovially, rising from his seat to shake Houdini's hand. "We are deeply indebted to Mr. Houdini for the happy resolution of this matter. I am glad of the chance to express my gratitude personally."

"I'm honoured if I have been of service," said Houdini grandly, giving a low bow.

"There now, that's enough of that," the prince said good-naturedly. "Do have a seat. All of London is awaiting your return to the stage. I'm only sorry for the unpleasantness of the interruption. But at least you came through it with your ribs in one piece, eh?" He smiled from Holmes to me. "Now, Mr. Holmes, we've seen how Kleppini got into the room, how did he manage to get back out again?"

"It may come as a surprise, but Mr. Houdini has explained that however impenetrable a safe may be from the outside, it is easily sprung from the inside."

"That's true," Houdini affirmed.

"Then why," I wondered aloud, "did Franz hire Kleppini at all? Surely Franz knew a good bit about locks from his years with Houdini; he could have broken out of the safe. Why didn't he carry out the plan himself?"

"Simply because Franz was too large a man to conceal himself in milk canisters or under tea-trolleys. He required the services of a much smaller man. Kleppini's known antipathy for Houdini made him the logical choice." By now Holmes had managed to get his pipe lit, and he sent a few curls of smoke up towards the ceiling. "If Franz had been a bit smaller we may never have solved this case," he admitted, "for it was Kleppini who sent the threat to Houdini which first drew us to the matter, and it was Kleppini who left the untenable pattern of footprints here in the study, and it was he who was finally tricked into repeating the crime. Hardly an auspicious criminal career!"

"Perhaps not," Lord O'Neill said worriedly, "but what are we supposed to do with him now that you've caught him? We can't very well bring him before a judge, suppose he tells what he knows?"

"The judge would find it singularly uninteresting," Holmes assured him. "I have questioned Kleppini closely; although he overheard some of your discussion of the papers, he never knew what they were."

"Then our secret is safe," said the secretary, casting an uncertain glance at Houdini.

"I'm very good with secrets," the magician told him. "It is necessary in my profession."

"I suppose that answers my questions about the theft, at any rate," the prince said. "Kleppini was brought onto the grounds in a milk can, wheeled into this room on a tea-trolley, and all the while everyone thought he was down in Brighton, owing to that aeroplane of his. Is that it?"

"An admirable precis, Your Highness."

"My blushes, Mr. Holmes. But tell me, where does Wilhemina come into all of this?"

"Do you mean the Countess Valenka?"

The prince nodded.

"The countess's murder is perhaps the most curious episode of this entire business. Watson"—Holmes turned to me—"when you spoke with the countess at the Cleland, did she say or do anything which seemed unusual?"

"Well, I hardly know how to answer that, Holmes. Very nearly everything about that afternoon seemed unusual."

Holmes nodded. "And when you first arrived at the hotel, you were told by Herr Osey that the countess was feeling unwell?"

"Actually, I spoke first with the countess's handmaiden. It was she who told me that the countess was ill."

"Ah, yes of course! The maid. But Herr Osey confirmed this?"

"Yes, he was extremely reluctant to give me leave to see the countess at all."

"Quite so," said Holmes, "quite so. But at length he was won over by your genial good nature, am I correct?"

"It was something of that sort."

"But before you were taken in to see the countess, wasn't there a further delay of some kind?"

"Yes, I was asked to wait while Herr Osey pleaded my case."

Holmes turned about slowly on his cane. "Watson, did it not seem irregular to you that Herr Osey was allowed into the countess's chamber when you yourself had such trouble gaining admittance? Where was the maid? Why did she allow any visitor to see her mistress in such a state?"

"It did seem peculiar, now that you've mentioned it."

"And was the maid present during your interview with the countess? No? Did she attend to her mistress or show you out? No? What would have caused her to be so remiss in her duties? The answer, I believe, is that she was at that moment far too busy posing as the countess herself."

"What?" I cried. "That doesn't seem credible, Holmes!

Do you mean to say I never spoke to the countess at all? It was the handmaiden all the time? I don't believe it! The girl's English wasn't at all good enough!"

The Prince of Wales cleared his throat. "Dr. Watson," said he, "I fear that what Mr. Holmes says is undoubtedly true. It was a deception which the countess often practiced. Her maid would entertain visitors, leaving the countess free to roam the city. The girl's feigned ignorance of English was part of the charade. The two women closely resembled one another and as young girls had been actresses together in the same company. When the countess married, she took her friend for a travelling companion. It pleased them to have this little game with visitors."

"Then, where was the real countess during all of this?"

"Dead."

"Holmes, that simply can't be! If the countess was already dead when I called at the Cleland, why on earth would Herr Osey and the girl try to convince me that she was alive? What would they hope to accomplish, unless the two of them were involved in the murder—?"

"No, no, Watson. It was not like that at all. Let us try to examine the problem from Herr Osey's perspective. In his view, the countess was merely unaccounted for, and had been for some time. I'm afraid that he suspected an assignation, rather than a murder. Hence, when you presented yourself at the hotel demanding to speak with the countess, Herr Osey believed that her reputation was at stake."

"Then this entire deception was staged to protect the countess's good name?"

"Precisely."

I thought of my surprise at finding Herr Osey at the Cleland, and of the heated exchange which followed. "Then he really is a gentleman, after all."

"Yes, he is," agreed the prince, "and he cared deeply for the countess. She was a . . . a very captivating woman."

"Well, that may be true," said Holmes, "but whatever her feelings towards you may once have been, Your Highness, she had resolved to allow your letters to be sold to a foreign power. Very much like a woman, I should say."

The man who would soon be George V stared sadly into his cigar ash. "I like to think she wouldn't have gone through with it," he said, "and still . . . who murdered her? Houdini's assistant, this Franz fellow?"

"Yes. I've no doubt he planned to do so from the beginning. He placed the body in Houdini's trunk in order to add murder to the list of Houdini's supposed crimes."

"Forgive me for interrupting," Houdini said, again bowing deeply towards the prince, "but this part just doesn't make sense. I can understand Kleppini holding a grudge against me all these years, but Franz? He was always my most loyal follower. Bess and I treated him as our closest friend. Now I find out that he wanted to see me put in prison, maybe even killed! I don't understand it, Holmes, what was his reason?"

Holmes regarded the American for what seemed a long while, evidently turning over a difficult decision in his mind. "You won't like what I have to say," he began haltingly. "It —it concerns your father."

"My father? How?"

"Does the name of the Baron Rietzhoff of Budapest mean anything to you? No? Very likely not. That was your assistant's real name."

"Franz? A baron? That's ridiculous! His name was Franz Schultz! His family was wealthy, but he was no baron. And he was from Stuttgart, not Budapest!"

"Yes, that is the story he told to Dr. Watson and myself as well." Holmes looked over at me. "Watson, do you recall what Franz said when we discovered the body of the countess in Houdini's trunk?"

"Let me see . . . something in German, wasn't it?"

"Actually, it was a Hungarian phrase. *Oh Istenem.*"

"Yes, that is a Hungarian phrase," Houdini said, "but Franz spoke Hungarian, German, English, and several other languages. He had a gift for it. I don't see what that proves."

"It proves nothing. I merely found it suggestive that a man purporting to be a German should use a Hungarian phrase so readily. Considering that you yourself are of Hungarian descent, I thought the coincidence warranted a cable to the Bureau of Police in Budapest. I received a reply only yesterday."

"What did it say?"

"Yes, Holmes," the prince urged, "don't keep us waiting!"

"Watson"—Holmes turned to me again—"after Houdini's arrest, we paid a call on my brother, Mycroft, at the Diogenes Club. Do you recall what he had to say about Houdini's father?"

"He said that Houdini's father was a murderer."

"That's outrageous!" Houdini cried. "I told you before, my father was no murderer! How can you say such a thing, and in front of the prince, too!"

"Calm yourself, Mr. Houdini," the prince said. "Dr. Watson was only reporting another man's opinion. He meant no offense."

"You're right, of course," said Houdini, remembering himself, "but you see, I grew up with that lie being spread all around me, and it simply wasn't true. My father did kill a man in Hungary, but he was forced into it in a duel of honour. That's why he came to America so late in his life."

"Houdini," Holmes said, tightly gripping the knob of his cane, "did you ever know the name of the man your father killed?"

The spark of comprehension appeared in Houdini's dark eyes, but he shook his head as if to deny it.

"That man's name was also Baron Rietzhoff of Budapest. He was the father of your assistant, Franz."

Houdini fixed his gaze upon his hands, which were clasped across his lap. "My father killed Franz's father?" he asked without looking up.

"I'm afraid so."

The five of us—the prince, Lord O'Neill, Sherlock Holmes, Houdini, and myself—fell silent, each of us lost in our own thoughts. I imagined the man I had come to know as Franz, now revealed as the scion of a noble house, plotting for years on end to bring ruin to the family of his father's enemy. Then I thought of Houdini, who had made a new life for himself in a new country, and who had known Franz only as a trusted worker and friend. How would Houdini reconcile the loss of his friend with this pervasive desire for vengeance, a vengeance directed against a family whose name he no longer bore?

After a time the prince cleared his throat awkwardly. "Hum! I've allowed my cigar to go out. Mr. Houdini, may I offer you one?"

"No, thank you, Your Highness," said Houdini, clearly preoccupied with other thoughts, "I never smoke. It would reduce my lung capacity."

"You don't say," the prince said bemusedly, pausing for a moment in the relighting of his cigar. "Then I suppose I'll have to curtail my underwater escapes, won't I?"

"I suppose so," Houdini agreed distractedly, stepping to the door of the room. "Gentlemen, please excuse me. I must return to the Savoy. Mr. Holmes has given me a good deal to think about. I'll need some time by myself."

"Harry," I called, struggling with my cane to get to my feet, "listen to me, please. You musn't blame yourself for what has happened. It really had very little to do with you."

He paused for a moment, staring at the heavy door of the Gairstowe vault, and then suddenly he became cheerful.

"Oh, I wasn't referring to that, John. I was talking about this business of sneaking Kleppini onto the grounds in a milk can. It gives me a wonderful idea for an escape! Imagine! An ordinary milk can filled with water! What an escape."

"It will create a sensation," I agreed.

"Oh, one last thing," he said more quietly, turning back at the door. "Please don't write about any of this business, John. Not while I'm alive, anyway. It's just that . . . well . . . I'd rather Bess didn't know the truth. I want her to think that Franz died while trying to protect me. After all"—he gave a broad wink—"the show must go on."

EPILOGUE

"LADIES AND GENTLEMEN, for my next escape attempt, I will require the assistance of a member of tonight's audience." Houdini stepped to the edge of the stage and peered out over the footlights. "Ah! I see just the man! My friends, this evening we are graced by the presence of an extraordinary man. A man whose wisdom and spirit guided me through my darkest hour, and whose tenacity and faith are largely responsible for my happy return to the stage. Dr. Watson, if Mr. Holmes can spare you for this one evening, would you consent to be my assistant, as well?"

Once again my fellow theatre patrons were more than kind in their reception of me, but even their warm enthusiasm moved me far less than the gracious words of Houdini. Making my way to the stage, I found my progress impeded by a sudden mist over my eyes.

"Thank you, Doctor," said Houdini, taking my hand firmly as I climbed to the stage. "It is appropriate that you should be by my side as I introduce to London, and to the world, an escape which defies all reason and yet is firmly grounded in the commonplace."

The orchestra music swelled to a grand crescendo as the rear curtains parted, revealing a disappointingly prosaic metal milk canister. The audience had by this point come to expect something on a rather grander scale from Houdini, so that this ordinary object left them decidedly unimpressed. Houdini seemed prepared for this.

"As you may clearly see," he began, "what we have here is a perfectly plain milk can, a fact which Dr. Watson will verify. You will ask yourself, 'What is so remarkable about this? Why should Houdini be afraid of a can of milk?' " The magician walked to the footlights and assumed a confidential tone. "It is true, my friends, that this escape may at first consideration seem to lack the subtle intrigue of my Walking-Through-a-Brick-Wall illusion, or the raw terror of my Water Torture Cell, but I ask you to consider further." Houdini's voice fell to a deeper register, which gave it an ominous shading. "A simple metal can. Barely large enough to hold a man. Once inside, even the smallest movement is nearly impossible." Houdini described the small space with his fingertips. "Now, a metal lid is clamped over the top and locked into place. There is no longer any light to see and precious little room to move. And one last thing, ladies and gentlemen"—Houdini walked upstage and laid a hand on the rim of the canister—"one last thing which seriously complicates my dilemma. The can is filled to the top with water!"

Houdini's dramatic pronouncement set the audience members to whispering excitedly among themselves. I myself doubted the sanity of such an undertaking as I watched Houdini's new assistants bring several large buckets of water onto the stage. The magician himself merely smiled at the excitement he had created.

"Think of it!" he cried, raising his arms to quiet the house. "It combines all of man's worst fears! The fear of confined spaces, the fear of darkness and"—here Houdini achieved the remarkable impression of having met every eye in the house—"failure means a drowning death! Ladies and gentlemen, for the first time on any stage, I give you the Deadly Riddle of the Milk Can!"

By now he had worked the audience into such a state that the very name of the effect produced wild applause, punctuated by several feminine shrieks. From the upper balcony a man shouted for Houdini to desist, which pleased the young American greatly.

"No! No, my friends!" cried the magician, again holding up his arms to be heard. "Though your concerns are justified, and the dangers great, I will not back away from this or any other challenge! This is what it means to face the dark spectre, this is what it means to chart the limits of man! This, ladies and gentlemen, is what it means to be Houdini!"

There then followed such a tumult of wild applause and shouting that it was several moments before the performance could continue.

To say that Houdini's return to the stage that evening had thus far been a triumph would be to do the great magician a disservice. His performance had been nothing less than miraculous, and his grip upon the imaginations of his audience had been masterful. For many weeks previous, the theatre sections of the London dailies had anticipated his re-emergence with great excitement, while in the forward sections of the newspapers, Houdini's role in the Gairstowe problem was detailed at some length. Even the ceremonies surrounding the coronation of the Prince of Wales as George V could not entirely eclipse the news and speculation about Houdini. All the while the magician had been content to avoid the public eye, revising and refining his effects and allowing the renewed interest in his doings to feed upon itself. Now, standing there beside him on that remarkable night, his first public appearance since the mistaken arrest and imprisonment, I could only marvel at how he had turned the near disaster to his personal advantage, propelling himself to the very fore of the public's attention.

Having overseen the placement of several large pails of water, a black folding screen, and the large clock used with his Water Torture Cell, Houdini turned to me and whispered, "I have to leave the stage for a minute, John. Keep them entertained while I'm gone, all right?" He slapped me on the shoulder and stepped behind the black screen.

Happily, the audience was still so wrought up in the wonder of the coming escape attempt that Houdini's absence was scarcely noticed. It was not until he reappeared a moment later, garbed in his bathing costume, that the house fell silent once more.

"All is ready," the magician announced. "As you see, my assistants are filling the milk can with liquid.* But before I undertake the challenge, let us try a different sort of test— one in which each member of the audience may participate. I will now enter the milk can and duck down below the surface of the water, but without locking the top into place. I invite each one of you to hold your breath along with me for as long as you possibly can. In this way, we'll see how each one of you might have fared against the milk can." Houdini stepped up to his waist into the mouth of the canister, splashing a quantity of water onto the stage as he did so. "Dr. Watson, that electrical switch at the base of the clock will start the hands. And remember, Doctor, I expect you to hold your breath, too! Now, if you are all ready, ladies and gentlemen . . . Begin!" Houdini slipped below the surface of the water as I started the huge clock. From the other side of the footlights I heard an enormous intake of breath as hundreds of the audience members endeavoured to outlast the young magician. I was something of an athlete at university, and I was always quite proud of the power of my lungs when swimming, but before even one minute had passed I was gasping for air along with most of the audience. In my case, I attribute my shortened

*Houdini used water in the can rather than milk for obvious reasons. Once, though, he let a local brewery fill the can with beer. He managed to escape, but he became rip-roaring drunk.

endurance at least partially to my nervousness at appearing onstage before so many people. Houdini, evidently, suffered no such stage fright.

Before ninety seconds were shown to have elapsed on the large clock, many loud gasps from the house indicated that even the hardiest of the patrons had been forced to take air; and before two full minutes had passed it was clear from the excited chattering all about the theatre that no one had managed to outlast Houdini. All eyes were now fixed to the milk can, but still the magician stayed below the surface of the water. As the hands of the clock reached three minutes, Houdini splashed upward out of the mouth of the can, his hands held high in triumph.

This feat of stamina won him a tremendous round of applause, which Houdini acknowledged by bowing deeply over the edge of the milk can. "Thank you!" he cried, struggling to regain his wind. "Thank you very much, you are very kind! And now—if you will allow me—the real test will begin! My assistant will now bring the lid to be locked over the mouth of the milk can. Incidentally, ladies and gentlemen, I would like to take this moment to introduce my assistant to all of you. She is my wife, Bess Houdini!" Mrs. Houdini came forward from the wings, wearing a fetching costume of violet silk. She was plainly delighted to have been reinstated as her husband's assistant, and she smiled warmly at me as she took her place by his side. "Thank you, Bess," said Houdini as he took the milk-can lid from her and held it aloft. "And now, once more I shall curl myself up inside the milk can. My assistants will then fill the can up to overflowing, replacing any water which has spilled out. Then my wife and Dr. Watson will fasten the lid onto the can, sealing me inside without any air at all. You have seen that I can last for three minutes underwater, but will I be able to escape from the milk can in that time? We shall see." Houdini paused here, standing waist-deep in the milk can, and gazed searchingly into the distance. "This ancient Celtic mystery was learned from a holy council of Druids who—" Houdini paused again, seeming to reconsider his words. I saw him glance up at the royal box, where the newly crowned George V sat smiling benignly. By His Majesty's side, in a chair generally reserved for members of the royal family, sat Sherlock Holmes. To the rear of them, in a position denoting what amounted to royal indifference, was seated the detective's older brother, Mycroft. As Houdini looked up at them now, his eyes seemed to frame a question, a question to which Sherlock Holmes responded with a slight inclination of his head.

Houdini looked back out over the audience. "My friends," he said, breaking away from his rehearsed patter, "my kind audience . . . many of you have read of my recent" —he searched for the proper word—"misunderstanding with Scotland Yard. Please be assured, I blame no one for the unhappiness, even though it nearly ruined my career. No, I blame no one." Inspector Lestrade squirmed uncomfortably in his seat in the first row. "Still," Houdini continued, "I would be remiss if I did not thank the two men responsible for setting the affair to rights. One of them you have met already, he is standing here beside me. The other man is also here with us this evening. He is Mr. Sherlock Holmes."

I would like to be able to report that Holmes blushed and averted his eyes, but in truth he rather liked public accolades, and most especially this one, led as it was by His Majesty the king, while Mycroft Holmes stared moodily at the floor.

"Without Mr. Holmes," Houdini continued, "my cause would have been lost. But he continued to seek the truth when all others thought me guilty of a terrible crime. The evidence against me was overwhelming, but Mr. Holmes was able to unravel it by focusing on what looked like an insignificant detail. Anyone else would have ignored this detail, but he seized on it and did not let go until it led to the answer he sought. This one detail, this seemingly unimportant aspect of a very complicated case, was ordinary milk. The milk which was contained in this very can. And my friends, just as Mr. Holmes recognized the importance of this ordinary can of milk and built it into one of the great successes of his career, so too will I. Mr. Holmes has shown me that there are great wonders to be found in life's commonplaces." Houdini paused and turned to me. "Dr. Watson, if you are ready . . . Bess . . . Your Majesty . . . Mr. Holmes . . . Inspector Lestrade . . . ladies and gentlemen . . . I now present the Deadly Milk Can!"

Houdini drew in a deep breath and slipped below the surface of the water. One of his new assistants came forward with a pail and poured water until the can overflowed onto the stage. Mrs. Houdini then clamped the lid over the top, fastening one side while I locked the other. Two more assistants placed the black screen around the can, shielding it from view. There now remained nothing to do but wait.

In my own defense, I must say that I began well. I recalled only too clearly my disastrous actions during that earlier performance of Houdini's, and I was not keen to repeat myself. This resolve enabled me to endure the first minute of Houdini's watery confinement with scarcely a qualm.

Even as the hands of the clock reached two minutes, and the audience began to grow agitated, I still remained calm, confident of Houdini's physical and technical skill. Had he not just shown that he could last three minutes underwater with no ill effect? Surely there was no cause for alarm.

But as the clock swept past three minutes I gave into my building sense of trepidation. By his own admission, Houdini had never performed this escape before an audience. Had it presented unforeseen difficulty? Could Houdini even move in the cramped space of the milk can, far less effect an escape? The audience's consternation had grown in volume and pitch so that shouts of concern were audible from every corner of the house. The danger was very real, I knew, but I had on that previous occasion seen him last four minutes before I made my dubious rescue. I would not make the same mistake now. And yet, what if my reluctance to embarrass myself cost Houdini his life?

At four minutes I began to pace a frantic line up and down before the black screen. As before, I saw the assistants shift about nervously, as if deciding on a course of action. But did any of them know the real danger? The man who truly knew Houdini's limits—the villainous Franz—was now dead. Was there anyone else who would recognize when Houdini's showmanship had crossed over into genuine peril? I looked about for Mrs. Houdini, but I could not see her.

Four and one-half minutes found the audience in a frenzy. The aisles were clogged with rescuers attempting to reach the stage. All about the theatre women swooned while men begged me to take action. More time had now passed than any man, even Houdini, could survive without oxygen. After all that he had undergone in those trying weeks, was my friend now to drown in a can of milk? I searched the royal box for guidance from Holmes, but his chair was empty. Frantically, I looked about in the wings for a sign from Mrs. Houdini. A group of assistants were clustered there by the edge of the stage. Surely they would put an end to it, surely they would unlock the hellish trap? I took a few steps towards them and saw, to my extreme horror, that they were gathered about the unconscious form of Bess Houdini.

This was all the impetus I needed. Performance or no, I would get Houdini out of that can before another second passed. Once more I dashed to the wings and seized the heavy fire axe. The din of the audience was now deafening, but I paid no heed as I pushed aside the black screen, showing the can still sealed.

One stroke of the axe knocked the canister to its side. I braced my foot against the neck and raised the axe high. Again and again I swung at the lid, first loosening the metal clasps so that liquid spilled out across the surface of the stage, then breaking them off completely, opening the can at last. Throwing the axe aside, I reached through the narrow opening to pull Houdini out, but I found the can empty.

I had barely a second to absorb this information before the spilled liquid had flown over the edge of the stage and into the recently installed electrical footlights. This resulted in a great, crackling flash of light, followed by smoky darkness. When the emergency gas came up a moment later, Harry Houdini stood beside me on the stage.

I shall never know how he managed it. Nor was I greatly concerned to know at the time. My first response was relief, relief which was echoed by the audience at a tremendous volume. But hard at the heels of that relief came the realization that I had once again compromised his performance and ruined one of his treasured pieces of equipment.

"Harry," I strained to be heard above the roar of the crowd, "Harry, I'm sorry about all this . . . it's just that . . . when I saw that Mrs. Houdini had been so overcome—" I glanced over to the edge of the stage and saw Mrs. Houdini, mysteriously recovered, standing happily at the side of Sherlock Holmes. Only a moment earlier she had been incapacitated with anxiety. It had been her prostration which impelled me to break open the can. How had she recovered so quickly? Why on earth was Holmes smiling so cannily? I cast a suspicious eye at Houdini, but he had turned away to acknowledge the cheers of his audience.

"Harry," I began again, "what—"

"Never mind, John," said he, bowing deeply to the royal box. "Think nothing of it. I never cry over spilt milk."

ELTING MEMORIAL LIBRARY
93 Main Street
New Paltz, New York 12561